I0692209

Chapter One

The coconut trees wave their branches as sexy women dancing to the beat of sweet Calypso music on a carnival Monday. Where else could such a thought be conjured up but in the head of a man who had tasted strong homemade wine, drunk coconut water and ate raw oyster seasoned with salt lime and pepper as an aphrodisiac.

The Country, where tourists learned to 'wine and jam' to Soca , Calypso, and Chutney music, attached to each other like vigorous spawning frogs swaying in an easy, upright motion. The birthplace of the Steel pan with its trance like sound that causes one to smile jump and shake.

Sensuousness grafted with heat, rum and spicy foods melting the so-called righteous behavior. Its hug me, jump with me, let me contort the body like a gymnast. Just don't stop the music.

A total body moving experience that shatters every ounce of inhibition and spirals one into an Afterglow of satisfied muscular contentment until limbs is hung over the bedside the next day. Documented and shelved in the secretive corner of the mind lies the bravado to resurrect at a moment's notice.

Yes sweet 'TnT', a shorten version of the name that both visitors and Trinbagonians fondly whisper when said. A cosmopolitan Country populated by 1.3 million people of whose indigenous folks were Amerindians. Imprinted in history is where the 2012 gold medalist Javelin Olympian came from. The island that was once settled by the French, Dutch, Spanish, Portuguese and conquered by the British. Its influences and dialects are now settled in the inhabitants of African and Indian decent whose journey began thousands of miles away with a sealed destination, stamped, 'Trinidad and Tobago'.

From the passing of sugar as mainstream revenue to Tourism and Oil it became the Americas of the Caribbean. Inhabited by a proud and friendly people who knew that even deep into the country side exists the elevator for higher education nestled close to waters that sing their own songs.

Beautiful beaches that welcome the Giant Leatherback Turtle to their bellies, whilst spectators stand in awe at their trails.

The mesmerizing call of the cicadas competes with the sounds of horny frogs fighting for willing mates-as the evening sky darkens like the spread of a changing blanket heralding the return of the corn birds to their wall free hotel. Meena smiled and drew her curtains as tomorrow was another day.

It was early in the afternoon and leaving Sangre Grande was a trip by itself. If you wanted to become vexed and frustrated, try to go grocery shopping on the last Friday in the month. That was the time when most folks have some form of a money matter to take care of, whether it be paying a bill, collecting salary, lime'in at the bar and having a few drinks or simply spending a little of it on a friend whom you haven't seen in a while. The grocery stores were always overcrowded and when it was time to get a taxi it was a real hassle.

It so happened Meena Rose's family including her sister Dustie, decided to get their groceries and do some shopping on such a day. The evening was absolutely glorious. The sun was out and yet it was not hot. You see, the town of Sangre Grande is situated close to a forest and somewhat near the Manzanilla beach even though it was approximately a half an hour drive away. So there was this constant breeze that kept the atmosphere cool at times.

The name Sangre Grande means Big Blood, and to this day she wondered what or who possessed that individual or individuals to give the town that name. The area had a country-like look with its large concrete houses and backyard gardens until you got to the main road.

In that location there were banks, stores, malls, restaurants, and so much more. The folks there were friendly since most of the time everybody knew one another. The population was about sixteen thousand and it was a mixture of people of different races. Whenever one saw a black woman with long, curly hair swinging on her back chances are it was hers, not a weave.

The town was surrounded by numerous villages and the folks usually converged on Fridays, causing a huge traffic and human jam. Most of these villages had shops, mini markets, seamstresses and hairdressers, yet the pull is to come to that little town. There was an overwhelming fascination that sucked you in. It is the magic of the 'lime'in', the hysteria of being caught up in watching persons move quickly to nowhere, the active gossip, noisy bars, laughter and the low secret whistle that the men gave. Sensuously calling thin women 'slims' and plus size 'thickness'.

All small villagers, as she calls them, herself included, looked forward to going to Sangre Grande. For them it's like a mini vacation among people you are either happy to see, will make friends with, immediately detest or never want to see again. It all depends on what happens on that day.

She always said that that place was hidden with mischievous-ness, mysteries, secrets and jokes. Don't be fooled if you see someone smiling all the time, that person could either be really happy to be there, half way drunk or raving mad!

That reminded her of the day she met Jake, a school friend, and was really glad to see him. The last time they saw each other was five years ago and they had a fun time together . So riding on those remembrances they had a fun time Meena went up to him and said 'hi' with a smile as bright as the sun light. She noticed people were staring curiously in her direction and she honestly thought they were admiring her sexy, low back blouse that had a jeweled spider web cut out in the center. It was unusual and she always came up with these fashion ideas for her seamstress that would set off a trend.

So feeling very proud she continued to talk to Jake. The more she spoke and reminisce the wider he smiled and laughed. She took him back to a time in school when they had to write an essay on 'planet earth' and he chooses to write about 'how Johnson lost his teeth'. The memory was hilarious and they indulged in laughter that echoed deep in the distance. It was only when he started to speak about a boat riding on an ant back and a set of incoherent 'mumbo jumbos' that she understood why he was smiling and what was the reason they were all looking in her direction.

The funny thing is, when you are innocent towards a matter or is not privy to certain information life is quite charming. You exist like a tumble weed just going with the flow, until reality registers.

In a split second her brain screamed, "What are you doing talking to that mad man? Don't you realize he is completely loco!'. Adrenaline said, 'jump backwards, heave and take flight' and that was just what she did. She literally took off at around fifty miles an hour around a corner and into a store to hide. She was panting like a dog on an extremely hot day with a pulse drumming in her head.

She never knew a heart could beat so fast. She felt it in her ears, mouth, throat, chest and back. That day she left the town in a hurry without taking care of any business matters. All she wanted was the safety of her home. You would think that would have put a stop to her romance with the town, but no no it didn't. The magnetic pull deepens its claws encircling her family like a sinking penny and that was why they were on their way there.

She got off close to the fabric store knowing she could never rush in to buy what she needed and hurried out. It's either she would meet up with Sherma, Nikita, Lucy, Beverly or some other friend who would keep her in some kind of old talk that could take the entire day to finish. Also, to buy fabric is a pain by itself. She would go into the store knowing exactly what is needed and by the time she got to the cashier her hands would be aching from the constant exchange of bolts of fabric, before her mind was made up.

"Meena!, Meena!" someone shouted as she was about to go into the fabric store. It was Ruby, and if she had seen her before she saw her, she would not have seen her dust. She always wanted to know your business and everyone else's so she pretended she did not hear her and kept walking.

"Meena, don't pretend you did not hear me because I know you did!" Ruby shouted.

"Oh, hey girl. I did not hear you," she lied.

"It's a long time I haven't seen you," Ruby replied.

"Oh yeah, but you saw me last week and you waved to me. Are you losing it girl?" said Meena laughingly so it would not sound malicious.

"Maybe, but the brain is not as it used to be these days. Remember we are getting old Meena," she said with mean satisfaction.
The look she was given translated the message and Ruby thoroughly understood.

"So what you are saying? I am the one that is looking old!" she retorted as she pointed to herself. Meena chuckled under her breath at the true statement.

"Whatever Meena! I don't care, because thoughts are just wind," she said with hand motions as if to wave the thoughts away.
She opened her mouth to speak, but hesitated, then said nothing for a while, as if composing herself.

"So what are you doing down here? You came to get fabric? You have a wedding to go to?" she inquisitively asked in one breath.

Meena wanted to say, 'shut up and mind your own business' but her mother always taught her to be polite and she have never forgotten it. So Meena chose her words carefully.

"Yes I came for some fabric, and no I am not going to a wedding," Meena calmly replied.

"You're looking really nice. You have a big job or what? I heard your husband is a big time supervisor on an oil rig.
You must be flowing in dough!" said Ruby in one breath again.

Ruby's eyes were raking her for news and she was a bit breathless with anticipation as her eyes fastened on Meena's hand bag.

"You have a real fancy bag there Meena. I want to see what you have in it," she commanded while reaching out to touch the bag. Meena hugged it closer to her body.

Meena's brain was telling her that it was time to end this conversation with Ruby because she was too nosy for her own good. However her lips said something else.

"Well my hubby works out there but that flowing in the dough is not as you think besides what's in my bag is for me alone to see".

Her brain said 'are you stupid woman? Why do you have her questioning you like that, get rid of her! Look at how she has you all flustered for nothing! This is absolute nonsense! Stupid stupid stupid you!'

By this time Ruby had blocked her entrance to the doorway.
"So you plan to travel soon? I heard you went to Margarita recently. Did you do plenty shopping?" she interrogated with a glint in her eyes.

Meena simply pretended she did not hear and pushed past her to go and examine some bolts of fabric that was lined on a shelf. She was fuming and her patience was running thin.

Ruby did not take the hint. She followed her inside and tapped her on the shoulder, a place she detested for anyone to touch her.

"So you did plenty shopping," she repeated, her tone of voice commanding an answer.

"Ruby Brown!" shouted Meena as she spun around. "What is it with you? You are too inquisitive! Are you an FBI agent or something? Why don't you go do your shopping and leave me alone!"

"You don't have to get on so! All I ask is if you did plenty shopping. What's so hard about that to answer" Ruby said with raw irritation tattooed on her face. Meena simply stared at her in total amazement.

"Ok Ok, let me go my way and leave all the big shots alone," she said as she stormed out of the store.

Meena was relieved when Ruby left and proceeded to take her time to browse through the curtain section of the store.

"But this was $5.95 a yd. last week and now it's $7.95! What they think miss, like we are spinning money from a spinning wheel or we are millionaires or something?" the person said directing her question to Meena.

"It seems so," she replied not lifting her head to look at the speaker.

"Meena is that you?"

She look at the person totally perplex not having a clue as to who she was. She searched her brain then it came back.

"Brenda? Brenda Luciano?" Meena said in shock as she recognized her school laughing partner who was now plus size like her and equally beautiful."

"Yes that's me," she said excitedly and they started to laugh.

"I haven't seen you in such a long time Brenda. Where were you all these years?" asked Meena as they hugged and kissed each other.

"I have been living in England but I am here now, here now," she repeated almost as a whisper as her eyes quickly masked something.

They laughed again and her infectious laughter triggered old memories.
"Remember how we use to laugh in school. It was you, Romie and I and she would always be the one to get caught," Brenda smilingly said.

Meena replied "I remember. Since she would laugh the loudest, the principal would send her on the stage as punishment where everyone would see her. From there she would give us the evil eye as if it was our fault she was punished" Meena was laughing hysterically.

They had to go out of the store for a moment until they were in a calm state.

Back in the store shopping madness took them over. Like a pair of possessed beasts, bolts of cloth were pulled shoved and searched whilst sweat cascaded down their faces. The snip of scissors added to the thrill of the moment as the fabric was cut.

Soon they headed to the food court to quench their thirst, eat and rest their backs. Meena decided she would sponsor the eats.

The smell of cooking roti and curry chicken tantalized the nostrils and excited the taste buds, making one silently hurrying the cook.

Meena stood in line to order their food and who could of slide into her seat but Ruby. She immediately waves Brenda a signal but she did not understand.

"What did you say?" she shouted as she cupped her ears.

Meena only smiled and waved since the eatery was packed with people talking, laughing, and shouting their orders with a child or two who was crying in the midst of all the confusion.

"Whom are you talking to," she heard Ruby asked loudly from the distance.
Brenda must have said who it was because Meena had to pretend; she waved and mouthed to Ruby if she wanted something.

Well it seemed that was the invitation Ruby needed. She got up and came over where she was standing.

Meena hoped if she said yes Ruby would remain sitting until she brought her food over to her. However that was not to be. She placed her order then told Ruby that she would pay for hers.

Ruby's request was different from theirs.
"Give me two bus-up shut with curry goat and don't play stingy on the kutchela, three doubles with tamarind sauce, one beastly cold carib beer, mmm a slice of sweet bread and an ice-cream cone

double scoop, Sour-sop flavor. Then let me have a tall milk shake," she said actually smiling. Her smile transformed her face to a spectacle of beauty that displayed a set of small pearly white teeth.

"I am going to have a chat with Brenda. You'll bring the eats," she said commandingly as she walked away with the milk shake.

Meena's brain screamed again. 'The nerve of this woman! Who does she think she is?'

Meena refuse to get close to where Ruby was sitting with Brenda but opted to walk around and admire the fishes in the tanks.

From across the room she heard

"Are you still living with Marvin?" asked Ruby.
She could not hear Brenda's response.

"You don't find he's too old for you? He is turning gray already." Ruby slurped the shake with a sickening sound.

Brenda said something again of which Meena did not hear.

"So how did you get that bruise on your hand? Did he beat you?" Ruby persisted.

Brenda looked frustrated and looked around for Meena. Meena stooped behind the fish tank and a few customers pretending to adjust her shoe strap so she won't be seen and called over.
A baby started to cry so loudly that she could not hear part of the conversation. As he quieted down she heard.

"He has no money! You mean he is poor? Girl! You must be joking. You need your head to be examined," she stated.
Brenda answered again and she still could not hear.
"Or, I wanted to know if you are so stupid to live with a man who doesn't have heavy cash". So where are you living now?"

Brenda answered casting her eyes around again for her. This time Meena was sitting slouched in a seat completely blocked by a group of young women waiting on their turn to place their order.

"Crescent Heights! You must be rich! Only rich people lives there. So how much bedrooms your house has?" Ruby asked, taking a final slurp from her shake with a contented look on her face.

Brenda answered massaging the back of her neck slowly. Meena was eavesdropping and she felt guilty not coming to her rescue but something inside her needed to hear more. Maybe she might hear something that will help her to understand that masked look Brenda had when they met earlier on, plus she now knew a lot more.

"So where he working?" Ruby asked, leaving out part of her sentence.

Brenda answered clenching her fist in the process.

"How much does he give you to spend weekly?" asked Ruby leaning forward as if to catch every word that was being said.
Brenda did not answer.

"You heard me, I said how much money he give you for the week!" she repeated in an interrogating manner.

"What do you want to know that for? Is that any of your business?" said Brenda aloud as she punctuated every word.

"No, is not my business but you could tell me. You afraid!"

Brenda started to laugh a sarcastic hysterical laugh.

"What's so funny? I didn't hear a joke" said Ruby sounding annoyed.

Brenda rose in rage with a red flush covering her face so Meena hurried over. From what she could recall about Brenda after a hysterical laugh, was usually a fight.

"So people, the food is going to take a minute. Meena smilingly said, trying to lighten the atmosphere that was charged with anger.

"They better hurry up because I am so hungry I could eat a horse," said Ruby completely forgetting Brenda already.

Brenda folded her left hand in a tight fist. Meena pulled her down in her seat as she sat.

"It's best I go and hurry them up," said Ruby ignoring the barbaric looks Brenda was giving her.

"What's the number?" asked Ruby directing her question to Meena.
"Number twenty six" she replied.

"Twenty six, twenty six you say," Ruby repeated to herself then cheups. She then got up and went to the counter to complain about their slowness.

"Meena did you hear what that skinny, scaly ghost was asking me? Why can't she stop questioning everyone she meets? I tried to be nice to her but she kept on going. I'm fed up now. She accuses me of living with Marvin! I am married to that man for the past twelve years. She's so fortunate you came when you did or else I would have floored that twig!" said an angry Brenda closing her eyes as they became tiny slits.

"Sh-sh Brenda". People began listening and watching. "Don't let her ruffle your feathers. She likes to get on people's nerves. Just play it cool. Just play it cool girl," said Meena trying her best to calm the tension.

Moments ago she needed that advice since she almost blew her top and here she was playing hypocrite telling Brenda to stay cool. Life was always so interesting.

"Ok Meena, just tell her to stay away from me," stated Brenda.

Meena rose and went over to Ruby. Her mind raced as she calculated that Brenda was still at school when she got married. She wondered if….. and her thoughts was interrupted by Ruby.

"What is she so mad about? I tried to make conversation and she is vexed like a big bull. People these days are so stupid. You think I am wrong to say that?" Ruby asked with an expression beseeching Meena to say no. At this point Ruby had incited her anger again.

"Ruby, where do you live? What are you doing in Sangre Grande today? How much money did your husband give you to spend? What do you have in your bag?" asked Meena hurling question after question at her hoping she would get the point.

"Husband, what husband! Anyhow what are you asking me all those questions for?" said Ruby in disgust.

Meena kept staring her straight in her eyes and when she realized what had just transpired Ruby excused herself to go to the bathroom.

"Number twenty six," said the clerk at the counter.

"Number twenty six," shouted Ruby as if she thought Meena was deaf. She said it on cue as she came out of the bathroom.

"You people had to grow up that goat or what! So long I had to wait and so much money I had to pay for that roti," said Ruby addressing the servers. Meena knew she was taking 'leave of her senses' when she said that.

She continued "I hope that goat taste as good as it smell or else you know me. It would be brought right back!", she said with an attitude surrounding the two last words as she picked up what was hers and placed it in her bag.

"Alright Ruby darlin" said the male server and she gave him a dazzlingly smile as she walked off licking her ice-cream cone.
Meena breathed a sigh of relief after she left.

"Have a nice day Ruby. We'll see you soon said Meena as she turned her back and went over to the table. She placed the tray down. But who again would pull up a chair sit down and annoy the ladies yet again? No one but Ruby, still attacking her ice-cream. Meena had had enough.

"What are you doing here Ruby? It's time you go and leave us alone" said Meena icily.

"Okay okay," said Ruby sounding irritated. "I just want five dollars to pay my cab fare. I would pay you back next week. I'm no crook Meena.

"You know it was never about the money. It's your attitude I cannot deal with," said Meena . Ruby looked at her with an expression that said 'hello! What are you talking about'?

Meena sigh, reached into her bag and gave her a ten dollar bill.

Ruby got up and asked "You all would be down here next week?"

"Yes and I will bring a big stick," said an angry Brenda.

Ruby stood up rolled back her sleeve and flexed her muscle for them to see. They were shocked to see such bulging muscles on her arm. She then flexed the other arm as if warning them, gave another dazzling smile and left.

"Girl you would not understand how she grates on my nerves with that attitude," said Meena.

"Since school days she was like that and she, have maintained the same 'Jekyll and Hide' personality. I think it's time someone told her how stank her attitude is. And you know what, she have the nerve to show her muscle as if we're afraid of that," said Brenda with a little doubt in her voice.

A lady came and sat at the table next to them and said "I was hoping she did not see me. She is my neighbor and she is real trouble. She left her husband and……….

Brenda and Meena looked at each other, got up and took a table for two close to the front where they could see the streets and hear what was going on outside.

"I wondered who was real trouble in this game," Brenda said and they both giggled like school girls. One look at the woman oozed 'gossiper' in capital letters and they weren't interested in getting caught up in that melee.

They didn't concentrate on Ruby and ruin the rest of their day. They had a nice quiet time and talked about their missing years and finally eat in peace.

The woman looked at them up and down then she emitted a long and loud cheups. The friends laughed uncontrollably and enjoyed themselves.

From that vantage point they could see what's going on outside, and to their delight a young guy was doing wheelie. He was actually showing off. He became more and more daring as he realized he had an audience.

"What is wrong with him? You see, look! Look! Look at that!" exclaimed a lady holding her head as the biker almost collided with a truck.

At first he was in the parking lot of 'the food court'. He did nice little tricks that had a gathering crowd that applauded and encouraged him to continue with his show.

"Mommy I want a bike to do that," said a little boy in the crowd.

"Me too," said another little boy.

"I want a bike mommy. I want a bike now!" said the second little boy throwing a tantrum.

"Could you be quiet?" said his mother as she adjusted her bag strap on her shoulder; for he had already pulled it off in rage. He then proceeded to kick his mother and threw away the frozen treat she had given him.

"Anthony what is wrong with you? You are not being nice. Please stop. You know I do not like it when you behave like that," she said very soft as if afraid to discipline him.

"I am not hearing you," he said as he stuck his fingers in his ears. "I said I want a bike!" he shouted to the top of his voice and he ran into the middle of the parking lot.

His mother seemed to get embarrassed so she went after him. At this point the cars that were trying to enter were not allowed in. This caused a traffic jam that ignited an angry set of blaring horns from drivers that did not know what was going on ahead of them. When she caught up with Anthony, she held him by his hand and he almost dragged her to the ground.

"How could she allow such bad behavior as if it was a joke," Meena said to Brenda. "Kids today have absolutely no respect for their parents or authority".

"Well if that was me, by now he would have been itching from a slap on those legs that he kicked me with. I don't know what it is with this generation today like they are born disobedient. Meena I cannot look any longer. Like that mother is foolish or something! No, no, no, I cannot believe what I am seeing," said a distraught Brenda.

The mother at this time was on her knees, her hand bag on the ground with its content spilled out and the baby on her side screaming to the top of its lungs. Somehow the baby got struck in the face by Anthony who kept kicking and screaming.

A woman in the crowd pushed passed everyone. A group of onlookers had gathered and each one vented their opinion as to what the mother should do.

"Why don't you cut that boy's tail! He is too small to behave like that and even if he was grown he still shouldn't. He thinks he is a man or something!" she said to the mother. "Look boy get up off that ground and behave yourself!. You need some good straightening out," she said angrily, directing the comments to Anthony.

Even the wheeler stopped his tricks and came over to see what was going on.

The woman said "Give me that baby and fix that boy!"

The mother handed over the baby, pulled Anthony up extremely close to her and whispered something in his ears.
Well, Anthony galloped into the air and shouted out "Oh mommy I won't do it again, I promise," he said dribbling.

"You see, that is what he needed to cool him down," said the woman as she handed over the baby and turned to a satisfied crowd whom were pleased about the discipline.

Who hit the boy, leave him alone!" shouted a young man passing on the side walk.

"Nobody hit the boy but if you want some, just come!" responded the mother with assertion.

"Miss I was only joking, pardon me," he said sensing there was more to that statement than he could comprehend.

The mother thanked the woman who held the baby for her then came into the eatery. There Anthony sat hugging and smiling up at his mother as she quietly spoke to him.

The wheeler then started his tricks again. This time he became so daring that he went into the street.

The woman who held the baby pulled out a cigarette lit it and blew a ring of smoke into the air.

"Look at that fool. He must have an appointment with death today," she said to another woman standing close to her.

"I can't understand it," she interrupted her speech to blow another ring of smoke into the air. The breeze swept the smoke straight into the face of a woman coming from the opposite direction.

"Watch where you are blowing your smoke" she said blocking her nose.

"It's a free country and I could blow my smoke wherever I want" said the smoker.

The woman cheups and walked pass the smoker then turned back and said "If God wanted us to smoke he would've put a chimney on our heads," and she continued on her way grumbling.

They both left the Eatery and started their long journey down the street. It was noisy, hot, and the sky was rolling in some clouds that were slightly dark in color.

"It looks like rain would fall today," said Meena.

"I hope not because I hung my clothing in the sun to dry and silly me did not listen to the weather report this morning," said Brenda.

"Well you know you cannot stop God's work."

"That's true," she said and pushed Meena to the side as the wheeler sped pass them with his shirt tail flying in the wind.

"Him again! Why doesn't he just go home. He is looking to make some kind of accident today. Mark my words," said Brenda seriously.
As she said that they heard a ' Bam!'

To avoid hitting a pedestrian, the young man had ridden on top of a slow moving car and he and the bike was now in the middle of the street. Fortunately for him, no other vehicle was coming in that direction.

The driver of the car came out fussing loudly. He said the young man was irresponsible because he noticed him playing the monkey for quite a while. A number of other passengers alighted from other cars to see if the biker was hurt or not.

"Are you okay. Are you hurt?" said a nurse who came out of a cab caught up in the traffic.

"Yeah I am good. Nothing is wrong with me," he said dusting his hands and feet as he got up.

"Felix! Felix!" shouted a strong looking man coming up the street.

"What you doing playing de fool whole morning on de street? Berthram told me he saw you and let me catch you, you would see where de barley grows. Your mother was looking for you whole morning. Boy what is wrong with you? I am tired telling you I have no money to bury you with this stupidness you're always doing!" he exclaimed.

Felix jumped on his bike and began to peddle as fast as his legs could carry him. He could not be bothered at that moment how twisted the bicycle wheels were, he was working it for all it could give.

The woman who had held the baby stepped forward and was talking to Felix father. Suddenly they heard

"Don't tell me dat Millie! He would get it when I get home," he said explosively. Millie continued to show him the antics of Felix and his bike while he swore.

All this time Brenda and Meena was standing in the sun sweating minding the people's business like typical Trinis. The sun peeped every now and then through the clouds. It had become humid, a sign that rain would surely fall.

They both hugged each other, and said they would call and meet up the following Friday. Meena heard a slight commotion and was shocked to see Brenda running alongside a car then jumping in as it sped off. She wondered what that was all about and what was Brenda really hiding.

Chapter two

Meena's husband whistled to her from across the street and she smiled as he gave her that enchanting look. He was absolutely gorgeous, tall, the lighter shade of black, a dimpled cheek and a beautiful set of teeth. She watched as he crossed with their daughter Ce Ce.

"Babes that was waiting in the doctor's office," he said looking a little bit frustrated. "It seems like today all parents brought out their children to see the specialist, so you could imagine children crying, mothers shouting and the constant digging in a box of toys in the office. The noise was like thunder!" he exaggerated as he held her hand. She squeezed his hand reassuringly letting him know she understand how he felt.

"Look at the traffic jam!" said her husband as he shaded his eyes from the sun. "Come lets all go and have a cool drink of coconut water."

Meena absolutely loved that drink. It was one hundred percent natural, tasty and loaded with vitamins a perfect pick me up that refreshed the soul.

That 'beautiful tree' she calls it is a fibrous rooted plant that can grow up to twenty feet tall. Their branch resembles the palm plant.

When the plant is about five to six years old it shoots these long pods that splits open to reveal a branch full of flowers that eventually turn into little nuts that Meena tried to count.

In about three months the nut was good for drinking. If left a little longer a thick jelly was formed that then could be scooped out and eaten. Some folks leave it to dry on the tree then it is used to make cooking oil, candles and soap.

Mothers love to massage their new born babies with the oil since the smell is fascinating and it moisturizes the babies' skin. The leaves can be used to make hats, mats, fans, and baskets.

The beauty is to see these trees sway in the breeze with their heads laden with nuts that's hundreds of times heavier than their roots and would not topple over. That's really cool, isn't it!

There is always a crowd around the coconut vender especially on a hot day. Their numerous voices could be heard two blocks away saying.

"I want two nuts pure water."

"Coconut man, one nut, light jelly."

"You know how long I standing here. Three nuts man! firm jelly. Like you don't want to sell me. My money doesn't have hair!"

Meena was still trying to figure out that part of speech.

"That is heat, phew!" exclaimed a woman fanning with her money.

"Well everybody have to wait because is only two hands ah have".

Chop, chop, chop, sounded the nuts as the vender skillfully opened it for complaining customers and collected his money as he handed over the drinks.

A new set of complaining was heard when the nut was drunk.

"Hurry and open my nut for me!"

"I want these three opened. Do I have to pay for that service too?"

"I am tired of standing. Coconut man you need to get another worker".

"Just leave me alone. De heat is enough to deal with," said the vender as he moved as fast as his hands could go. On such occasions no one said "please" or "thank you" because everybody was under the impression he or she was waiting too long.

Their daughter Ce Ce was dancing to the sound of the chopping nuts as her husband stood waiting patiently on his turn.

"Yeah man, what you want," said the vendor to her husband.

"One water, two jellies," answered Leon.

"You alright miss?" he said to Meena as he caught her sweating profusely. "You would enjoy this, it is cold and sweet."

"Thank you," she said taking the nut from him. Meena thought she was a disaster but an old man was gulping down his in gasps. His shirt front was wet from sweat and coconut water.

Drinking coconut water from the nut is an art. You've got to put your mouth precisely to the opening or it would spill down your chest.

The old man had leaned upon the side of the van enjoying his nut with a bag full of grocery attached to his arm. One could see how uncomfortable he was but he was not going to put down that nut until it was done.

"You're okay pappy?" asked Meena's husband.

The old man only smile and continued to suck on his nut. When he was finished he said "Yes!" with great satisfaction and wiped his mouth and staggered away. Her husband chuckled as the scene played out itself.

Meena on the other hand always a little social, never like to put her mouth to the nut since she did not want her lipstick to come off. So she asked the vendor for a straw. They usually had them but would keep them hidden for reasons she couldn't understand to this day.

Whilst enjoying her nut she heard:
"So that is the husband. He mixed or something?"

Meena's hair on her neck stood on its ends because that voice belonged to one person, RUBY!

She wondered how that woman could have seen her. The glare was so strong that Meena had to squint until she could hardly see and she was in a little shade. Ruby's eyes barely existed yet her eyes missed nothing. For Meena that was a mystery.

"Is this your daughter? She has really pretty eyes, like they are blue gray. I really did hear so," she stated as Meena ignored her.

"Look at parcels! Meena you are a shopaholic!" she exaggerated for there were only two.

"Let me see what you have in them," Meena completely ignored her.

"Meena, is this your friend?" ask her husband politely.

Her brain said 'friend? Man you must be crazy! This woman irritates the day light out of me! Just chase her away!" But her lips were silent.

"Yes we are school mates and my name is Ruby" she answered.

"It is nice to meet you. I am Leon," he said.

"So are you married a very long time?" asked Ruby.

"Pretty long," answered her husband.

"So are you happy? Well you all look happy," Ruby said answering her own question.

"You work out on an oil rig?"

"Yes" answered her husband and looked at Meena. His look said 'why is she so inquisitive? Meena's brain said 'don't look at me. It was you who decided to talk to her. Please just get rid of her' Yet again the lips were silent.

"Would you like a nut?" he asked.

"Yes thank you," she said sweetly with a dynamic smile.

"Coconut man give her a jelly and water please," said Leon.

"Only open the water and I want that big one up there," she said pointing to a large bunch of nuts which was stacked way up on the truck.

"Those in that bunch have firm jelly miss," said the vendor.

"That's better. Just shave it, and do it good because people like too much short cuts these days.

"Lady, look, take your nuts and don't bother my soul this time of the day" said the irritated vendor who had to delicately climb on the bunches to get her specific nut.

She took her nuts and cheups .

"Are you my aunty?" Piped their little daughter Ce Ce.

"No she is not!" Meena finally found her voice.

"Yes I am." Ruby sang the words tauntingly.

"I am aunty Ruby, honey," she gently said when she spoke to their daughter.

"Aunty Ruby where do you live?" ask an innocent Ce Ce .

"Not far away from here," Ruby replied very quietly casting her eyes in Meena's direction, hoping she did not hear her reply.

"Do you live in a big house?" ask Ce Ce .

"Well, kind of," she answered, hesitating and looking quite uncomfortable.

"Ce Ce, it's not nice to question anyone about their business," said Meena's husband as he scolded their daughter. "You have a nice day miss," he continued" and we'll see you around sometime again."

"Ok bye!" she said and beat a hasty retreat.

"My my what an inquisitive soul, Meena. You meet all types these days," Leon said under his breath.

Her brain was on a war path of mischievousness that day so she did not listen to it nor did she respond or it was going to get her in real trouble.

"Open your nut ma'am?" asked the vendor.

No thank you," said Meena. Her appetite was gone and it was all due to her accusing brain that kept telling her what she was supposed to and should have said, at the time. Also it seemed like she was a target only to be irritated by Ruby. It seemed when the opportunity came to give Ruby a tongue whipping, she said nothing so she must have been stupid. Meena was totally confused at that moment so she cheups. It was so loud that even the coconut vender stop chopping a nut to find out if everything was okay with her.

She put on her brightest smile and let everyone know she was fine even though her brain was now saying 'liar, liar, and liar.'

When Ce Ce was finished eating her jellied nut, Leon suggested they first go to the bank then the shoe store to which she agreed.

"Where did Dustie and Emma go?" she asks him.

"The last time I saw them they were heading toward the seamstress. Dustie said she had to collect some dresses from Nola," said Leon.

"Whom did you say, Nola?!"

"Yes, that's what she said."

"Well she is very brave to go there."

"Why do you say that?"

"The last time I went there she ruined my outfit. I did not realize she used to drink to such a state of intoxication."

But was it not her who made that sexy green suit I like to see you in?"

"Yes it was her and she has also sewn many nice pieces for me. However lately she's been drunk. I do not know what is wrong with her. For Dustie's sake I hope she did it well because we have that anniversary coming up and she bought a special piece of fabric to make her dress."

"Don't worry your head too much honey. Everything might turn out good," Leon said reassuringly to Meena as they strolled towards the bank.

Chapter Three

From the distance they saw Dustie standing at the entrance to Nola's sewing shop. Her body language told all was not right. As they got closer their daughter Emma came running towards them.

"Hi mom hi dad" she said.

"Did you have a nice time with Aunty?" asked Meena.

"Yes I did. Aunty got me a toy and an ice-cream," said Emma.

"I want a toy and an ice-cream too," said Ce Ce.

"Aunty would buy it for you ok CeCe," said Emma as she hugged her sister.

"Aunty is angry mom really angry," emphasized Emma.

"Meena could see the veins that stood on her sister's neck and that was a sure sign that she was thoroughly disturbed.

"What's up girl" she asked Dustie as she came closer.

"She (Nola) sews one suit and spoiled it. She made the top small enough to fit a flea," Dustie exaggerated. The thing is, she knew I was coming and she is not even here .Her apprentice showed me the dress and just looking at it I was already mad. I am waiting here to fix her. If she knows what's good for her she would buy back my expensive piece of fabric and I am taking back everything she has for me!"

Everyone stood in the shade and waited for Nola. All this time Dustie was fuming about the situation. Around ten minutes later Nola came, slightly staggering from a bar across the street. At that precise moment a woman who was standing at the side of the shop suddenly emerged and blurted out:

"You Nola! You're a drunk. You think I am picking up money from the ground. This is the third piece of garment you've spoiled for me this month. And where you think this could fit? Look at my size and calculate in your brains if this was going to pass my hip?" she shouted as she held up the garment. Anyone could have seen that it was too small. The lady was around a size twelve and the out fit looked two sizes smaller.

Nola just stood on the walkway with a stupid grin on her face, sucking the liquor from a bottle she had concealed in a brown bag.

"Woman!" shouted the disgruntled customer, "I want my money back and right now...." She dropped the garment on the ground and made some advances toward Nola.

"Excuse me miss," interrupted Leon "why not wait until she is in a better frame of mind to discuss it. No good would come out of this right now. Just look at her. She is barely coherent," he said anxiously as Nola was trying to say something that could not be deciphered.

"You are right mister. She is not good for her self-right now. I'll come back tomorrow real early. You have ah nice evening," She picked up her bag and outfit and left.

Dustie had to assist Nola inside. Her anger had receded. She politely asked the apprentice for her bag of fabric and they left.

Silently Meena promised herself to return and speak to Nola when she was sober. This was a woman who made brides dresses; as a matter of fact she sewed for everyone involved in weddings. She had acquired a good status in life from her profession. She had built a beautiful home from her business and when she spoke about it you could've seen the joy emanating from within her. She also had a big sewing establishment where she wholesaled certain items.

But it was a little over a year she has been reduced to a small shop with a few machines. Some of Meena's best and sexiest, and more exotic pieces of clothing Nola personally sewed for her. To see her fall from grace like that was sad, really sad. She needed to know if there was something she could do to help her get back on her feet again. Also she wanted her seamstress in her life.

Chapter four

They were happy to get to the bank. It was cool and welcoming. The air-conditioning was just right. Five tellers were operating so Meena thought they would be out in a blink.

The line stretched almost to the door and took two turns around some plants. Her husband and sister joined the line and Meena got a seat as a lady got up. She was fortunate since a lot of folks were standing hoping to get one.

A man was sitting in a chair close to her so she said to him: "I find the bank is extra overcrowded today."

"Yes, it's fortnight , plus end of month so every fox and its mother comes out at this time," he stated.

"Have you been waiting long?" Meena asked making small talk.
"Yes around one hour now this is quite long. Like those tellers need turpentine under them

to move fast. This bank is good but it is the slowest and I only stayed with them because it's easier to get a loan here. I have my space in front that lady in yellow over there," he rattled on.

She looked over to where he pointed and saw two ladies in yellow, one stood behind the other. As she turned back to him he whispered softly to her:
"The one with the big feet and bobby toes."

Meena immediately looked at the plus size lady's feet which was not the right one. You know how society has people trained that even her; a plus size became a target. Imagine two women standing there one thin one plus sized. Why didn't she just look away. Then the line moved a little and she saw the lady's feet.

This woman was short and petite with giant feet. They actually looked like Hobbit's feet. Meena did a double take upon seeing it. The lady had on a laced up yellow Roman-like sandals that immediately called attention to her feet. Each toe was polished in bright yellow that could be seen from a distance.

Two women were laughing uncontrollably in a corner. Meena did not see anything funny about that because if the woman was proud of her feet then let her be.

Ce Ce who was six years old left where she was and went walking along the line of people and saw the lady's feet.

"Mom, Mom," she called out.

"Yes honey,"Meena replied

"Why is the lady's feet so big?"

"Ce Ce," Meena shouted "come here now!" By this time Ce Ce was bending over looking at the lady's feet.'

"Dad, dad, da-ad!" she shouted at her father who was engrossed in a conversation with the man behind him.

"Yes Ce Ce, how may I help you?"

"Why is the lady's feet so big," she shouted again.

Leon left in a hurry got Ce Ce and apologized to the lady. When he brought her over his eyes were dilated in shock.

The bank became quiet except for the two women who were now low to the ground stifling their laughter.

The lady was truly embarrassed so Meena had to do something. She got up put her other daughter in the seat took Ce Ce and went over to the lady.

She said to Ce Ce :

"Look at mommy. Am I not bigger than this lady?"

"Uh huh," she said

"Am I not taller than this lady?"

"Uh huh," she said

"Do you like my red sandal?"

"Yes mom they're nice"

"Aren't her yellow sandals nice also?"

"Yes they resemble your yellow shoes."

"Isn't she a beautiful lady?"

"Yes she is."

"So what if her feet are a little bigger than mommy's. Aren't hers nice also?"

"Uh huh,"

"Now you must always remember what I taught you about being different." So everyone's feet are different and remember daddy have big feet also. So don't go pointing or shouting if you see someone looking different to you.

Then Ce Ce laughed her childish laughter and repeated what her mother said about her father. "So you go say hello to the lady."

CeCe said hello and offered her a candy which the lady took and said thank you.

By this time the two women had stopped laughing because it was not funny anymore.
Meena came back to her seat and her husband winked at her whilst showing her the peace sign.

The man next to her said: "Impressive miss, very impressive."

"Thank you," she said feeling good that she used her initiative to defuse a sensitive situation.

"Next, next," said teller number five.

Number five belonged to a young man who paid more attention to a lotto ticket than his turn on the line. He had a bunch of them and was oblivious to his surrounding.

"Man move up in the line! I say move up!" shouted a man way to the back of the line.

"But he must be deaf or something, boy move up!" said a lady with a high pitch voice.

"Look you see me I am passing him," said the woman with a beautifully styled head wrap. And she began to inch past him.

"Where you going?" said the young man then he continued, "You better wait your turn."

"But you know how long they are saying next, next, like you're deaf or something!" said the lady.

"Move it" said a strong looking guard as others began to complain.

"What scene you're on brother man? Everybody saying move it move it like they belonged to a band or a chorus," he replied as he went up to the teller.

"Good day princess," he said to the teller then he gave her his bank book and withdrawal slip.

"Bunch of hooligans. Always cramping black man style," he hurled at the crowd in the bank.

"Oh shut up!" shouted the woman with the high pitch voice.

Two guards came forward and every one got quiet.

"Thank you princess, stay as sweet as you are," he said to the teller as he blew her a kiss.

"I am de Champion they call me de sweet loto man" he sang out loudly as he put on his twisted shades and swaggered out of the bank showing the power sign.

This erupt a peal of laughter from the crowd, even from Dustie who was exceptionally quiet since they left Nola's shop.

Chapter Five

With their wallets filled with money, everyone was quite happy again. Meena spoke particularly about Dustie. They had the same euphoric feeling that took over when they were about to spend money. Dustie had eighteen hundred dollars in her purse and Meena had fifteen.

They both smiled when they heard how much each other had. Their minds worked almost the same way. They had already seen the avenue to borrow from each other, in case their money ran out.

Her husband walked ahead with the kids as the ladies became engrossed in conversation. As they walked along the way their conversation waned out to become more focus on the immediate mission. There it was: the new shoe store that had opened a week ago. They rushed inside and her sister Dustie made a beeline to a section with an array of sexy three inch high heeled sling back gold shoes. She was very slender and always looks great in high heels.

Meena was looking for the wide with section. There was a specific shoe she saw advertised in the showcase. She became so absorbed in her search that she bumped into someone. It was Beverly. She turned around and said : "Oh it's you" in a sarcastic manner.

"Hi Bev, how are you?" said Meena completely forgetting about the long running feud between Bev and Dustie. She had nothing to do with what happened between them and here she was smack in the middle of it.

"You brave to talk to me," Bev stated.

"What are you talking about?" asked Meena in all ignorance.

"Remember Dusty said I feel I am so sexy, and I am out of place and nosy for minding her business whether she ends her name with an ie or ty" said Bev sounding hurt.

"So what if she said that. Aren't you sexy? Her name, a different story, that's her business however she wants to end it" stated Meena.

"Of course I am sexy, but she said I am always wearing mini and showing up my legs for all to see.'

"Okay, you tell me; don't you always wear a mini and show off your legs?

"Not all the time. When I go to functions, it's on my knees, actually for my sister's wedding it was to the ground."

"Bev, life is too short to worry about small things. Meena really wanted to say ' things like that' but it was a big problem for Bev at the moment.

"Did you hear Joey died?" Meena was trying to swing the conversation away about Dustie hoping she didn't hear them.

Unlike Meena who many times would remember what their mom told them both over and over again, 'when you observe a situation becoming volatile, back off, and never forget it takes two to make a quarrel.'

Those words passed through one of her sister's ears and out the other. Very rarely she gave up her right and almost never back down from a quarrel. So one could understand why Meena quickly wanted to change the subject.

"Do you remember Joey Samuel?

"Yes, he was the handsome curly hair guy with the dimpled chin who used to sit in the third row three classes up from us" Bev stated being very informative.

"Yes that's Joey" replied Meena, wondering how Bev remembered all those details.

"I liked him a little, however when I realized he was a womanizer I left him alone. Someone really told me he had contracted the HIV virus and I did not believe it. Unfortunately when I saw him about a year ago he didn't look well. It's such a sad situation. How unfortunate for such a beautiful man," her voice trailed off. She became absorbed in her thoughts. Meena was about to move off when Bev said :

"Look at me. Although I wear my mini, no unsavory character, handsome, rich, or poor could make advances and I succumb. I know I have nice legs and I flaunt them."

She looked at Meena like she could read the expression on her face.

"Come off it Meena. Look at the type of eyes you have: always made up nicely and look how pretty you are. Then your voice, remember from since school days everyone complements you on it. You mean to tell me you don't flaunt what you have!" Bev said both shocked and amazed.

"I think you …well you are correct to a certain point," Meena hesitantly said. She could not play a hypocrite on this issue because honestly, she took extra care of herself and played up what she usually got complemented on.

You know Bev we are living in dangerous times now so people do not have that love for one another anymore. So you got to be careful. It's safer not to excite those no good characters in our society who have nothing good up their sleeves. Do you agree with me?"

"What you are saying is right Meena. Even my mother was telling me that sometime ago."

"Aren't you tired of standing? Let's go sit over there." They both sat, with Bev trying to pull her micro mini skirt down that refuse to budge. She then held her bag over her legs for a little coverage.

"Girl" Bev said seriously. "One month ago I came home from a party around two o'clock in the morning. When the cab dropped me off, I saw two guys hiding on the side of an abandon house, two lots away. The light from the taxi reflected on the building and I happened to look back for no apparent reason and I saw them. As I started to walk up my driveway they came out into the street. I felt fear. It's a good thing I called my brother and asked him to look out for me. My driveway is very long. Anyway as they reached it, I started to run. My brother was in the verandah and I shouted his name and he came out with my dog Frico, who ran past me down the driveway barking. They were up to no good because as soon as they heard my brother's voice, they ran."

She looked visibly disturbed when she was finished speaking. That story bothered Meena and sent her mind back to what she saw with….

"Bev again I say you've got to be careful," she said sympathetically while holding her hand.

"I know," she said "I have already slowed down on my late partying and I now wear jeans whenever I'm out late. The taxi brings me home. He takes me up the driveway straight to my front door. So I am taking all the precautions I could for the while."

"I know you work the shift system. What happens when you leave work that late?"

"I drive, I bought a nice Red Madza," she excitedly said. She continued "My mother waits in the veranda for me and recently we have put in security lights."

"Look at us. We are supposed to be looking for shoes but here we are talking about something else," she said bringing the subject to an end.

"Yes shoes ,shoes shoes! I want size nine, a wide with," said Meena while pulling her thoughts back together. Bev pointed her in the direction where she could find them.

"Meena I am so happy you had forgotten about that incident or else we would not have had this wonderful chat. Could you say hello to Dustie for me? I realize from now on her name is her business" said Bev sounding quite relieve.

"Sure I'll do that," Meena said, half truthfully not knowing whether or not she would tell her.

"I have to work tonight so we will catch up along the way" she said getting up in a hurry.

"Are you still working in the Maternity Ward?" asked Meena, with a slight smile gently lifting the corner of her mouth.
"Yes, and you know how busy that ward is, and the screaming ladies"….. They both laughed while Meena remembered her delivery. Bev was one of the attending nurses and she was one of the screaming ladies.

She then located Dustie. She had three pairs of shoes and was looking for a fourth. With excitement written all over her face she picked up a green pair and playfully said: "Come to mama."
That girl was more messed up than she thought.

"Dustie are you buying all these shoes?"

"Yep," she replied not even looking in Meena's direction.

Meena just sighed and moved on to look for her stuff. She took them over to her sister who said they were nice without even casting an eye in her direction.

"Dustie are those shoes your size?" ask Meena quizzically.

"I have not tried them on as yet but I think so."

"Could you do it now? It is almost time to go. Are you sure those shoes are your size?"Meena asked yet again.

Dustie took the first pair and tried it on but her heel would not go in. She repeated it with all of them, all ending with the same result. She then sat down and stared at them.

"Are you going to get a bigger size?" Meena foolishly asked.

"I can't understand why they don't fit," said Dustie in a puzzled manner.

They go through this every time. Her sister refuse to believe she wears size eleven and a half in shoes and would always try to squeeze her feet into a size smaller than what she should wear. Depending on the make some times it worked. So Meena went to the shelf and got her sister sizes that would fit her. Dustie picked them up and sighed as they paid for their purchases.

Across the street from the shoe store people were gathering around a truck. Dustie touched Meena's hand and pointed to the truck.

"That looks like the tangerine vendor over there," she said

"Oh yeah, lets go and get some. Looking at the truck closely Meena said, "It looks like the man I buy from".

They hurried across the street. The backed up traffic began creeping along the road. Horns blare as other cars came out of the side roads, pushing their way into the line. The walkway was extra crowded with pedestrians competing for space with their bags and baskets filled with all type of goodies. Vendors of all kind usually line the street edges selling their fruits and vegetables at prices everyone look forward to on a Friday.

It was never smooth sailing for people to get what they wanted from the vendors. People pushed all the time to get the best the vendors had to offer. Meena gave Dusty the parcels to hold and dove in. She had her huge, single braid nicely secured in a bun with a flower gracing the side of her face. When she came out, she was minus the flower, the braid was hanging down her back, and a lady's glasses stuck in her hair. But who cares? Meena had gotten some huge tangerines to be shared between them.

Now where in the world was Dustie. As she searched, she found her standing almost a block away near another shoe store, looking angry. As she got closer, Dustie, in puffs of restrained anger, yelled "Hah! Lord, "Hah! Lord," and each time she shook her head.

"What is the matter Dustie?" she asked nervously dreading the reply.

"Hah! Lord," she said again. "You wouldn't believe what just happened," she said in a disbelieving voice.

Meena was curios plus a little bit anxious. "Just tell me," she said impatiently.

"I am under strain with all these parcels in my hand trying to get here. Guess who showed up? Meena watched and listened to the rest. "Ruby, she was being her old self yet again. Why is it she always want to know what's in everybody's bag? Is it something with us or with everybody," she said, sounding frustrated and highly strung.

After Dustie calmed down they were able to get their parcels in the cubicle that were set up outside the grocery store.

"Hello there nice ladies," said the bag clerk, winking at Dustie and showing off a set of gold teeth.

"The gentle man and children are already inside," he said, addressing Meena.

"Thank you," Meena said in horror as the bag clerk was massaging her sister's hand while she handed him the bags. The next moment his hat was in the drain, ripped off by Dustie and thrown there.

"Have a nice time shopping," he said in a shaky voice, directly towards Dustie who barely acknowledge him. Everything happened in a split second. Meena began to doubt it ever happened.

Chapter Six

In the supermarket the girls were armed with their shopping cart. It was fun. Their duty was to find the cereal, powdered milk, Milo and Ovaltine. CeCe drinks Milo and Emma loves Ovaltine. Meena could never understand why because for her, the both drinks taste the same.

"Remember the day CeCe's Milo was finished and we tried to trick her by giving her some of Emma's Ovaltine," she asked .

"Yes, that was trouble," said her husband(Leon) smilingly. "CeCe, for whatever reason, knew it was not her drink and threw a tantrum that morning.
"Here comes CeCe," said Leon with a chuckle".

She was struggling with a huge can of Milo.
"Mom, I took this one cause I do not like Em's Ovaltine, and you know that", said CeCe. There she stood trying to look all grown up and looking for approval.

"Okay baby," Meena said and CeCe smiled that cute grin.

"Mommy, mommy," shouted Emma. "They have some big fat smoked herrings and it looks like they're filled with eggs!" she exclaimed with excitement.

Everyone in the lane and who could see Meena and her husband was staring at them. Most people ate smoked herring but it was a hush hush thing. When Meena was growing up, she would ask for the herring quietly in the hopes no one would hear or see her, especially her friends. It was always the talk and joke of the day. The irony was that most families always had it for dinner.

It was considered the poor man's meat and rightly so. It was only the (let me say) not so rich people's houses that dispelled the onslaught of olfactory twitchers that perfumed up the air with it every evening . Smoked herring had a distinct smell and people used to roast and prepare it however they wanted. While they cooked, the entire neighborhood knew what you were having for dinner. And please do not roast it in the house because everything would smell of pure unadulterated herring. Roast it on a wood fire outside the home and pray the wind didn't blow.

One may wonder why bother to go through the trouble if it had such a stigma. Well it tasted so absolutely delicious. After roasting the bones were separated and skinned from the flesh. If there were eggs, one would be in for a treat. In those days it was considered ('the not so rich') caviar. People used fresh coconut oil, lots of freshly sliced tomatoes, onions, sweet peppers, lemon or lime juice and hot pepper. This would be eaten either with fresh roasted bake, dumplings, dhal(yellow cooked peas flavored with cumin) and rice or ground provision commonly called 'roots food ex. (yams eddoes etc. etc.) Nowadays it's a treat for the tourist, like 'hops bread(round puffed bread) and fried shark.'

Meena's mouth watered as she thought of it. Dinner would be cornmeal dumplings and smoked herring. So all eyes were on them.

"Come and see the fat smoked herrings with eggs. How many packs do you want mom?" Emma shouted.

"Five," said CeCe, showing her sister her fingers.

When society has molded the thinking of folks certain way it was amazing (not in a good way). Here Meena was embarrassed to answer the child because she still didn't want people to know, that she eat smoked herring when the majority of folks did it.

"Emma, we're coming," said her husband, sensing Meena's dilemma.

"Can we get it?" insisted Emma.

"Not as yet Emma. Go get your marshmallows," he said diverting their attention away from the smoked herring. They both left and hurried away to the candy section.

"Why does this child have to shout so loud? My goodness! Couldn't she be a little bit quieter?" Meena said to her husband, under her breath.

"Honey don't say that. Remember we never taught them to be shameful about anything. And so what! Everybody eats smoked herring. Those two ladies over there that were looking at us probably eat it themselves," he said in an authoritative voice.

She saw the humor in what he said and bend over in laughter as the two women pushed their carts in the direction of the shelf filled herrings. Her husband joined in with a delightful chuckle, especially when one of them snatched two packs and quickly hid them under her groceries.

Chapter Seven

Meena's basket was filled when she joined Dusty in the line at the cashier. During the time they were in the store the rain had come down in showers. The traffic had eased up and the streets were flooded.

"Look dad, look" said Emma, shaking his hand to get his attention.

"There goes tomatoes and cucumbers sailing down the river," she said happily.

Meena knew a vendor was not happy because his produce was being washed away.

"Here come mangoes. One, two, three, ten . Oh my there are so many to count," said Emma clapping as she skipped numbers.

Lots of people crowded the entrance to see what was happening. This was the talk of the hour; everyone gave their opinions as to what was taking place.

Her sister was mumbling under her breath but she pretended not to hear her. Dustie did it for a while, casting little hopeful glances thinking Meena would ask her what the matter was all about.

"Right now I feel to buy some frozen chicken. Look at the condition of the street I have to go across to get my fresh chickens. If I did not have friends coming over on Sunday, I would leave that bird right where it is," Dustie said, sounding frustrated.

Fresh plucked chicken was the must for their family. It was a theory that if the chicken was frozen, it is stale and no good. On Friday afternoon, or early Saturday morning the meat was bought fresh from the poultry store.

They usually chose the cocks and considered themselves an authority on chickens. They encouraged customers to buy cocks because they swore to have meatier thighs. Their mother trained them that way. However she never bought hens and they have continued the tradition.

After the birds were plucked and feathered, the customers chose the freshest herbs and spices to season the meat. There was usually a fine feather left on it that has to be synched off, slightly roasting the outer skin in the process. When the meat was cooked, it had this unique flavor that could never be gotten from a frozen fowl.

"Hon," Meena said to her husband, "when the rain eases a little, could you go get the chickens for us please?" Meena's brain was saying 'm'mm the satisfaction of eating fresh plucked chicken marinated and cooked in fresh herbs and spices is so delicious.' At that moment she did not care if her husband had to cross a flooding street as long as that plucked fowl was in the basket to take home.

He looked at the water in the street, his shoes, then at her, and said: "I'll see".

When the rain stopped, the water in the streets seemed to disappear, as if by magic, and the hustle and bustle started all over again. Her husband quickly joined the crowd crossing the street to get to the poultry shop.

The sun came back out in all its glory and the vapor began to rise. Soon it was humid again. People were fanning and complaining about how the rain came down suddenly and how the sun was too hot the heat was killing them, blah, blah, blah. Complain, complain, and complain was all that could be heard at that moment.

"You really can't please people," said a lady passing in a hurry. Papa God do his work and everybody complaining," she said to no one in particular. Then the unfortunate happened. She took up a slide and went running into the crowd knocking down two men in the process.

"Ha, ha, hah," laughed a man standing close to Meena.
"She too busy talking and not looking where she was going. "Ha, ha, ha, ha, ha" he laughed again.

Meena also found herself shaking with laughter tickled by the infectious sound the man made as he exploded in varying waves of connecting crescendos.

The lady was helped up by others who also fell. She proceeded to give the man who was laughing uncontrollably a verbal assault. This only incited his laughter to a higher pitch. She told him his turn would come soon and when it did she would kick him and roll him in the dirty water.

Dustie leaned against a wall and laughed until she cried when she heard what the woman said. Meena was afraid that the lady might see her and mistakenly believe she was laughing at her so she took the kids back into the supermarket.

The evening was drawing to a close and everyone was tired and needed to go home. The children were sleepy, fussing and complained their legs hurt. Meena comforted them as best as she could but getting a taxi was not an easy game. Each time one stopped the rushing patrons were ready to pull those still seated in the car, out.

"What happen ! So what is this! You all want to break off my car door! Everybody will get home. I can't understand what all dat(that) rushing is all about" said the driver in broken dialect .

Two passengers were allowed to be seated with the driver. When the taxi stopped they would disembark and two more would get in. This time a rushing client allowed only one to alight and slid in blocking the other patron from getting out.

"Hey what is this!? Man get out and let me get out!" shouted the passenger.

"Are your ears deaf or what? Open the door and let de(the) man get off! You know something you get out an doh(don't) come back in!" shouted an already irritated driver.

The man got out let the passenger off and slammed the car door so hard that it sounded like an explosion, which gave Meena an instant headache.

People always made life more difficult for themselves. Life would be so much nicer if people acknowledged their wrong doing. The man made it difficult for himself because the word spread around and all the other cabs he tried to board told him no.

"It's time to get out of this town girl," said Leon as he left them and went in the direction the taxis were coming from. Lo and behold! a taxi pulled up with just him in it.

Her brain said 'Meena what is wrong with that man of yours, is that the only cab he could find to put you in? Are you getting in? If you do then you must be crazy.'

Her husband hailed the guy who put the groceries into the trunk and within minutes everything and everybody was in including Meena.

Meena however did not want to get in the cab. This cab was driven by a man nicknamed Snail. If one had an emergency, Snail was not the person to get you there. Lorette, her neighbor was pregnant and suddenly went in into labor. She and her mother left with Snail. His name tells you the whole story. Lorette ended up having the baby in the car and the ambulance had to come and get them.

When he left Sangre Grande, he usually doubled the time any driver would take. He would always say: "When the rain falls and the road became slippery, I take my time and don't want anyone to hurry me up."

Any other day it would have been fine with Meena. The drive to Manzanilla was most interesting and scenic especially for those who admired nature like she did.

The flowers were always in bloom. The greenery was soothing. The drive through the orange and grapefruit fields, with the yellow and golden fruits, was fascinating to the eyes. Not forgetting there was always someone standing by the road side to wave at. But today was not one of those days.

The taxi crawled along the road so slow that Ruby was able to see her in it. Ruby waved at her and said "See you this weekend." She had a terrible headache forming since the car door was slammed. Meena glanced back at Ruby. She was surrounded by a mountain of parcels and she wanted to know what she had in them. As if on cue Ruby blew her a kiss. Meena jerked her head around so quickly that she actually took the headache up another notch.

Dustie saw it all and she exploded into laughter scaring the driver so much that he bucked the car. This just added insult to injury. She closed her eyes as they slowly went home.

Chapter Eight

Have you ever been awaken by the sound of chirping birds? Well Meena had and it was the most pleasant experience. That euphoria stays with you most of the day. It was Saturday morning and it was beautiful. The chirping birds had awakened her. They were having a feast eating fruits and oh so noisy. As she lay in bed, the aroma of freshly baked bread filtered into the bedroom adding to the nostalgia. The girls were chatting with their dad in the kitchen. Even her headache was gone.

The sound of vehicles zipping to Manzanilla Beach punctuated the serenity that greeted them this particular Saturday. There was going to be a festival where prominent Soca artist would be featured. Many town folks were trying to get ahead of others to have prime parking spots. When such an event occurs thousands attend so being early was always a plus.

Meena came out and sat in her veranda to observe what was going on. Numerous vending trucks were racing to occupy the right spot. An estimated nine thousand or more persons would be jamming on the beach in a few hours. The entire night before, vehicles came up with people who camped out for the party next day. Manzanilla had seven miles of beach so there was room for every one.

On the main road, villagers put up stalls to sell their mangoes, coconut water, oranges and whatever they think folks would be interested in. An aroma emanated from her neighbor's kitchen and she knew it was kurma they were frying. When the neighbors are finished, they would send some over which is crispy, hard and delicious. However one must have good teeth to eat it.

As Meena enjoyed the early morning breeze, her dogs began to bark. It was the 'crab catcher', checking his traps for the night catch. His face and head were wrapped with cloth with only space for him to see. His arms were covered with two layers of long sleeve shirts and he also had on long pants and tall boots. He had to dress this way since mosquitoes also occupy the crab holes and were always looking for a meal.

Big juicy crabs(blue backs) made their home along the river banks or sometimes they would come onto peoples lawns. It is Meena's belief if crabs could make their home on her lawn they belonged to her. But the crab catchers didn't seem to understand that because they had no boundaries.

One day, not too long ago, two men were in a heated argument over that same situation and she had listen on.

"But you cannot just walk into my yard and set trap to catch crabs without my permission," said the one man.

"The crabs are not yours. I did not see any name written on the crab back," said the catcher, in a boisterous voice.

" Man you understand what I am saying. You leave quite by the river to come quite to MY step to set up traps to catch MYcrab! Look around, do you see any other crab hole?" he asked, punctuating his words with a raised voice.

"But I said the crab is not yours," said the catcher, beating his chest as he said the word 'I'.

"You are greedy. You looked to see if it was a big crab and you believe I shouldn't have it."

"So what! Crabs are free and I would take them, where ever they are," said the catcher.

"Well brother man not here no day no way! Get out of my yard!"

"Oh now you wanna push man!" said the catcher challenging him.

"I don't have to touch you. I don't want to touch you because if I do I would get myself in real trouble," the man said seriously.

The catcher started to move out of the yard.

"Hello, don't leave your trap here! Take it if you want it," the man stated.

"So what you will do? Destroy it?" asked the catcher, challenging him yet again.

"Exactly!" said the man.

"You try if you brave enough," said the catcher brandishing a machete he had in his hand.

"You think I am bluffing? Well watch me," said the man and he jumped off his steps down into the yard.

The catcher dropped two of his traps and leaped into the bushes on the other side of the road not even looking back. He was only full of steam.

The man took the trap and hit it against his house post smashing it to bits.
"You'd better not come around here again," he shouted.
There was no answer. The crab catcher was long gone.

Traps were set all along the edge of the man's lawn. He went down and shook out all the crabs from the traps into a crate then he threw the traps on the other side of the ravine (small stream). He then looked across someone's house.

"Hi Lauren, do you need help shaking out those from your trap?" he asked.

"No thank you Isaac. He took them already and it didn't bother me since I do not eat crabs. What angers me is that they steal my oranges and limes when I am not here," she stated.

"All you have to do is stop them from coming unto your property," he advised her.

"I have a 'No Trespassing' sign up but that doesn't seem to work" she complains.

"So what are you going to do to solve that?" he asked.

"I have already bought wire fencing to fence around my yard," she said.

"Good for you. I am going to get two dogs with lion heads so when they bark they will scare the shirts off their backs,' he joked and they all laughed.

"Well neighbor, tomorrow it's crab and callaloo (delicious soupy dish made from the leaves of the dasheen plant) for me," he said as he waved and went inside.

The crab catcher came on her lawn setting traps and aggravated her dogs that were very territorial. He came along not by himself but with a bunch of other dogs
.

Meena had to do something or her little dog Roxy would either end up with a heart attack or no voice when this was over. He was a mixed of Dash Hound and Mongrel. His little feet were very short and his body was long as a sausage. How that breed came about she didn't know but the lady that gave him to her said that was what he is.

She stood up and one would think the crab catcher would leave her premises. No he didn't. He came right up to her rose garden and set up a trap, not even acknowledging her. At this point Roxy was barking lying down and no sound was coming out of him.

"Hello, excuse me," Meena said but the crab catcher pretended not to hear her.

"What are you doing?" said her husband with his great booming voice as he went out into the yard and picked up Roxy.

"You are not leaving some for me?" said Leon as he soothed Roxy.

"Yeah, yeah" said the crab catcher.

She did not know if he understood or misunderstood what her husband said.

"Do you have a pan or something?" he asked.

"Yes," said her husband.

The catcher opened his bag and put around eight juicy looking crabs in it for him.

"Thanks man, and how's the catching these days," he asked making small talk.

"Good, real good. You see those traps down there," he said pointing to the edge of their lawn, "You could keep it for the girls," he said.

Both Emma and CeCe heard what was said and screamed in delight. Meena on the other hand was quite please how things worked out. The catcher left happy with a bag filled with oranges that her husband gave him.

Chapter Nine

At one o'clock someone rang the door bell. It was Dustie all dressed up and ready to go to the Soca Jam(festival where artist sings).

"Meena ,you're ready?" she asked as she came in singing a calypso.

"Ready for what?" Meena said, just teasing her.

"Girl you must be crazy!" Dustie said as she pulled her shades off, believing her sister was serious.

"CeCe, Emma, your aunt is here," Meena shouted to the girls.

"Hi aunty," they replied running out to meet her halfway dressed.

"You had me going there for a moment Meena . I thought you were serious. Sh! Sh!, listen listen to that tune," and Dustie started to dance encouraging Emma, who had the rhythm, to dance calypso.

A number of vehicles had stopped with patrons crowding a stall on which there were huge arrays of things. The villagers looked forward to the festival as it brought along lots of buyers thirsting for fruits, delicacies and homemade wine.

The wine making was Meena's husband special project. He sets his wine two years before it is sold so it was aged, strong, and kicked like a horse. He sold six different types of wine. Cinnamon and orange was the favorite. He had set up his booth next to a mango vendor who sold eight different types of mangoes. As the mangoes went so did the bottles of wine. By the time they were ready to leave, Leon had sold out all he had, while people still asked for more.

They all left, dressed in white tops and jeans pants, except Meena who had on a red halter that tied in a large bow in the back. She felt the red against her chocolate brown skin was sexy and no one dared contradict. On the way they met up with friends going in the same direction. Everybody's driveway was crowded. Even empty lots were turned into parking space with an attendant. All eating parlors were crowded and every other house had a barbeque going on by the road side. Blaring horns, laughter, music and the aroma from food greeted the people as they came closer to the beach.

Dusty was whale'in like her waist was rubbed with snake oil. Leon was chipping(slightly dragging feet movement) to the music while their daughters were following their aunt. Meena stood and waited for a special song to breakaway like her sister. The rhythm suddenly took her husband over and, throwing caution to the wind, Leon grabbed her and they started to dance true Trini(Trinidadian) style.

It was sweat, heat and excitement. They were enjoying themselves to the max. The crowd gathered around and the laughter was explosive each time the dancer did something that entertained the crowd. Meena was having such a good time that she didn't realize what had happened. Some folks moved from a vantage point to get a little closer and got some drinks. Meena seized that opportunity to rush her family to the spot they had vacated.

From there they had a bird's eye view of the stage and everyone around within a certain radius including the dancer in the middle of the ring. Meena began to dance then suddenly froze. She was stunned. Her heart leaped in her chest. There she was standing in the middle of the crowd. It was Ruby.

She was dressed in a slinky fitting tiger color outfit and was gyrating to the beat of the music. Her upper body was very muscular and her hips were slender .She had large breast and the outfit was hugging them. She was dancing wild and the crowd was caught up in it. Meena felt like a spy but was drawn to look at her. Ruby changed her movements and it became slow and hypnotic while she smiled and played the crowd.

Ruby had a lovely rhinestone studded hand bag that went over her right shoulder and hung on the left side. Each time she moved, the sun light bounced on it blazing kaleidoscope of colors surrounding her in mystery. Meena wondered what she had in that bag and wished she have gotten a little peek inside it. She felt a guilty flush covering her as the thought raced through her mind.

Ruby turned and was doing antics facing in Meena's direction and she hid behind her husband. Now what was the matter with her, she thought. She came to have a good time but here she was hiding from someone who probably did not even see her. She danced back to back with her husband took little sneak peeks every now and then to see what Ruby was doing.

"Dusty," she whispered but she did not hear her.

"Dusty," she spoke a little louder.

"Yes?"

"Look down there".

"Where?"

"In the center of the crowd".

"I am not seeing… you mean the guy having a good time? You know him?"

"What guy? Look again."

"Is everything ok baby?" asked her husband.

"Yes. Everything is cool with me," Meena answered.

She sneaked a peek and it was really a guy dancing now. Meena stopped and sat down complaining it was so hot and she was so thirsty. Her husband took the hint and left to get them drinks.

As soon as he was out of earshot she said to Dustie:
" Do you know it was Ruby dancing in the middle of that crowd before that guy came on!" she said in total disbelief.

"You're sure?" Dustie said doubtful.

"I really thought you had seen her".

"No I didn't. But where could she have gone?"

"That I would like to know," said Meena, as her eyes scanned the crowd.

"Don't let that upset you. We came here to have a good time and we're   not going home until then," said Dustie, with a chuckle forgetting Meena for the moment to get up to dance.

"I won't let her interfere with my day," she said to Dustie, who acknowledge by smiling. She had the notion her sister did not even hear her. And of course she lied. Her eyes searched the crowd for Ruby inch by inch and she was upset she did not see where she went. She finally came to the conclusion she probably had left.

The artist on stage struck up a song that had everyone clapping. A thunderous applause went up each time a person finished. One by one they sang, treating the patrons to a melody of tunes. There was an intermission and Steel Pan players entertained.

They had phoulorie(delicacy made from fried seasoned curried dough), ice cool watermelon, hops(round puffy bread) and shark. Towards the end of the evening Meena and Dustie had their hands around each other and they were chipping down the street. Dustie then saw someone she did not see for a long time. They stopped and she went over to say hello.

Someone touched Meena from behind. A voice that aroused her anger said:

"I see you had a good time. I didn't know you eat hops and shark. I like it too with plenty pepper," Ruby said, with a soft chuckle.

Meena turned around slowly and she was gone. She saw her moving swiftly through the crowd with her hand in the air waving to a catchy song that played from a truck parked at the road side.

Meena's brain said, 'Now why did you take so long to turn around when she spoke? Are you afraid of that woman or something? You keep saying you won't let her disturb you, but if you ask me that is a blatant lie. Just give that woman what's coming to her, because I do not understand what game she is playing with you. I am tired of seeing her put your emotions on a roller coaster. If you know what's good for you, you will do it soon '

She wanted to reply 'yes brain' but two ladies was standing close to her and if she did they might of thought she was mad or drunk so she gave her sister a sign to meet her at the sugar cane stall instead.

As Meena walked over out popped Ruby from behind a car coming straight towards her. She was prepared for her this time. She was going to let her know how she felt and what she thought of her and her inquisitiveness. Finally Ruby's day had come. She stood her ground looking her straight in the face as she came towards her. Meena felt like she had grown a few inches taller with anticipated reckoning, however, Ruby passed her straight and only whispered, 'nice bag'.

Meena felt drained as built up energy became deflated. It reminded her of lifting an aluminum pot with the strength for an iron pot. And what is this fascination they have for each other's bags? In a blink when she came towards her, Meena felt the urge to snatch Ruby's bag and rip it open to see its hiding contents. She was a quiet hypocrite and that was a secret she had to keep.

Chapter Ten

Situations happen in life that could make a person laugh, cry, or angry. Meena was disturbed. What was it about Ruby Brown that had her always wanting to know people's business and to see what was inside their bags? Now Meena wanted to see what was inside Ruby's bag. Nobody else's but Ruby's.

Evidently she had to go way back. She enlisted her sister to go with her to visit a teacher who taught the three of them in school. No way were they going to reveal the reason for their visit so it had to be carefully planned- not to arouse suspicion.

They called him up and were told it would be a pleasure to see them after so long. Their intention was to stay for two hours get information and get out. Somewhat like an FBI move.

So after a few days of planning they arrived to the smell of baking cookies and cakes. Mrs. Sealey was at the door to greet them.

"Welcome girls," she said.

Meena was surprised to see a much younger woman than she had anticipated.

"Now tell me who is who?" she asked quite friendly.

They introduced themselves and she hugged them. Meena immediately liked her and judging by the way her sister smiled, she knew she felt the same way too.

"I have prepared a lovely day for you all until Mikey comes home. I see you look confuse but Mr. Sealey's first name is Mikey," she said.

'Until he comes home! This is high class nonsense! I need information badly and he is not here!' Meena's brain screamed.

But as usual her lips said:
"We had expected him to be here. He's not going to be gone for the whole day, is he?" she asked.

"I hope not. He had to take care of....,"her voice trailed of and she sniffed.

'Now what was this,' thought Meena, feeling a bit awkward. However she said nothing but sat in a comfortable chair by the window.

"I am sorry," said Mrs Sealey, looking really sad. It almost prompted Meena to ask her what the matter was.

"Excuse me one minute," she said and looked quite happy again. Mrs. Sealey got up took out the cake from the oven, put in a pie and chicken to bake, brought out a jug filled with freshly squeezed orange juice poured it into three tall glasses filled with ice then sat down.
Meena picked up her drink and emptied half of its content down her throat, moisturizing the dryness she felt there. Mrs. Sealey slashed three thick slices of cake which she shared around then sat again. She began to flick imaginary dust from off her blouse front and wiped the table for the umpteenth time looking all absorbed in what she was doing.

"Now Mrs. Sealey, what was that sad face about?" asked a slightly impatient Dusty, who was fed up with the stalling.

"Well girls you all seemed to be honest and good and I appreciate nice company. I have a secret and no one knows about it. It has been burdening me for quite a while and I think it's about time I should tell someone.

What was that, is it a car?" asked Mrs. Sealey

"Yes," said Dusty.

"So what is it you want to tell us?" she asked trying to hurry Mrs Sealey up in speaking.

"You see Mr.......is that a car door that closed?" she asked Meena since she could see straight on the outside from where she sat.

"Yes, its Mr. Sealey and he is coming up the driveway with lots of parcels in his hands.

"Could you go and help him for me please girls?" she asked, with besieging eyes.

"Okay, but don't forget what you were going to tell us," said Dusty sounding a bit impatient.

"Go quickly girls," She hurried them off, completely ignoring Dustie .

"I cannot believe the unfortunate time he chooses to come home," whispered Dustie under her breath.

"Such bad timing. I wonder what was it she was going to tell us," Meena whispered back, as Mr. Sealey came towards them.

"Oh hello, Mr. Sealey. It's nice to see you".

Please let us help you with those parcels," said Meena, as she took some from him.
He looked good for his age and his dyed hair made him look even younger.

"Dusty and Meena James," he said as he hugged them. "Well I know you are not James anymore," he said directing his comment to Meena. He continued "You both look the same way as in High School. It's as if the clock stopped. I remember you all as little tots; now look at both of you," he said, with a chuckle.

"Oh yeah! Well thank you Mr. Sealey," said Dusty as she winked.

"You have such good memory Mr. Sealey, do you remember everyone else from high school?" Meena asked, trying to seize an early opportunity to get around to the subject, or rather the person she had in mind.

"Not everyone, but I do remember the majority especially those in your grade since I had four students from that class that won scholarships. No more talk about school for now. I want to hear about the both of you. Dusty what about you and that temper? Have you learned to control it?" asked Mr. Sealey, as he opened the kitchen door to let them in.

As they entered, Mrs. Sealey latched her arms around his neck and kissed him with teary eyes telling him how much she loved him. What a show of affection Meena thought to herself. This was so nice to see because these days society hardly ever shows public feelings like that.

"Oh honey," he said blushing and kissed her. He then removed her hands from around his neck and held it.

"She does that everyday. You see the reason why I am still alive today," he said.

"Oh please Mr. Sealey! With a memory like yours, you would live forever," Meena playfully said.

"Thank you Meena. Please don't try to fool an old man," he said smiling then continued, "I see you all had the pleasure of meeting my beautiful wife, Lisa."

As he said that, Meena saw Mrs. Sealey jerked her hand ever so slightly away from his. It was almost undetectable-she kept on smiling as she went to get him a glass of juice.
His eyes followed her for a while then he turned his attention to Dusty.

"So Dusty , I am waiting for your answer," he said as he pinched the tip of her nose.

"Yes sir, good enough. Temper is under control sir," she said quite convincing.

Meena's brain laughed, 'hah,' then it said, oh please! You need a good whipping still. Temper under control- nonsense!'

It was actually three days ago while she was visiting her, that vendors came to buy coconuts. Dustie has two acres of land cultivated with oranges and coconut which she sells. She told them do not pick from a particular tree close to her house.

The nuts on that tree were large and yellow and one of them could fill a twenty fluid ounce jug. She enjoys drinking those instead of water. Plus the tree was not tall so it was not too difficult for her to get them.

Meena did not know if the vendor did not understand her or he was downright greedy but Dustie caught one of his climbers swinging down an enormous bunch of her precious nuts. She flew into such a fit that the climber literally shook from fright. She stopped them from climbing, took away her large bunch of nuts and grumbled for the days that followed.

An orange vendor who did not know what took place stopped at her gate, and before he could ask a question she chased him away and became angry with her Meena for laughing at the situation.

She knew her sister had to remember that latest incident because it caused a little rift between them. Since then she let her know that the whole situation got out of hand because of her uncontrolled temper. Now there she was telling Mr. Sealey it was under control.

"Well that's so nice to hear because I heard about your marvelous achievements when I met up with Dana Steel," he said.

Dana Steel was one of Dustie's friends in whom a bad bone was not found. She was an extremely pleasant person and one would never have to worry if she said anything about anyone since it was always good.

Mr Sealey hurriedly drank his glass of juice and invited them to see his backyard. They went through a corridor then down a flight of stairs that opened into a beautiful garden.

There was no way such beauty could exist in such a little space, but it did. The proof was before Meena's eyes. Huge red roses lined up on a short walkway with pink and white periwinkles at their feet. He had a grafted black and cream rosebush that blossomed in its glory. He was proud to show them an array of orchids that dazzled their senses.

"Mr. Sealey, this is absolutely fantastic," Meena said.

"Come," he said smiling, motioning them around a bend where a small hanging garden was located. Its beauty was priceless. He took up a basket and went around a short wall decorated with creepers. Behind it was a neatly tucked away vegetable garden. Dusty held the basket as he picked two large and healthy looking heads of lettuce, some tomatoes, scallion and string beans. Meena felt like Alice in Wonderland.

"Taste this," he said and handed them two big plums from a miniature tree.

Dustie devoured her plum but Meena kept hers since she was afraid that bugs had crawled on it. He also had oranges, limes, and mangoes.

'This is almost out of this world," Meena whispered to herself in wonderment. She honestly felt she could pitch a little tent and live out there. For a while everything was forgotten-even the purpose why she was there.

Mrs. Sealey called and they went inside. Lunch was just almost ready so they helped to make the salad with the fresh produce from the garden. After they ate they were ushered into a room filled with rocks of different colors and sizes on shelves. Mr. Sealey told them his wife was a rock collector. That was a surprise because she seemed more like an artist. There were no signs to suggest that but Meena's brain chose that category.

When they were comfortably seated, Mr Sealey said, "Tell me about yourself Meena. What are you up to now?"

"I'm up to, nothing!" she quickly defended herself, completely misunderstanding his statement and feeling embarrassed since she was actually really up to something.

"I meant your achievements in life, your career, things like that," he said with a slight puzzled look on his face.

He sat quietly and listened attentively to all she had to say, moving his head slightly in acknowledgement. It transported her back to school days and she was moved to tell him she had finally begun to take singing lessons.

Dusty had disappeared into the kitchen with Mrs. Sealey. Mr. Sealey chuckled, then said: "Singing was not one of your strong points; it was math and biology. However I know you would master it someday," he encouraged.

He knew her strong points since he was her teacher. The opportunity presented itself for her to swing that conversation in the direction she wanted it to go. Meena began to call names of persons who were in the choir, deliberately mentioning Ruby Brown.

"No, she was not in the choir," he said.

"Are you sure?"

"Yes I am, I remember she was not there. I knew them all. Have you forgotten I was one of the stand in choir teacher?"

She did not forget, but she had to play that game.

He called the names of all the other students, some who had tried out for the choir that she had forgotten about. Then he said:
"I think I have pictures of you all somewhere."

At that point Meena was so anxious that she shook. He brought out an album with a picture that was taken on picture day of all those who were in her grade at that time and there she(Ruby) was, pushing a little girl as the picture was taken. As she looked closer she recognized Dustie and Ruby was squeezed in next to her. She quickly turned the pages and found one more picture with Ruby holding her hand and Dustie stood a little way off looking sad. There were pictures of their second grade class but Ruby was not there. She asked Mr.

Sealey about it and he told her she had moved away with her father but had returned.

Meena remembered she met her up in the school corridors and she would always avoid her. What she did know was that Ruby was in regular fights with girls, all bigger than her whom she would beat up.

He sat up in his chair then said :
"She was extremely secretive and would not let anyone look into her book except for the teacher. She kept her bag with her at all times and would never let anyone see into it".

"So what did she achieve in school," asked Meena.

"Oh she was a smart kid, and won a scholarship the year after you left. I knew she had studied marine biology for a while but then I lost touch with her" said Mr Sealey.

"How long ago since you last saw her?" asked Meena.

It's been years I haven't seen nor heard anything about her. One thing though: when she has it in for you, maybe jealousy or fascination, she becomes another person," stressed Mr Sealey.

Meena shivered a little and wondered if Ruby was a psycho or a stalker. She shook her head as if to shake off the thought before it took root.

She left Mr. Sealey rocking in his chair half asleep and tiptoed to the kitchen. Dustie and Mrs. Sealey were so engrossed in their conversation that they only became aware that Meena was there until she cleared her throat.

The conversation ended abruptly and Dustie said: "You don't worry, just stick to your plan."

Half an hour later they each left with a cake and promised to keep in touch. Mr. Sealey was sound asleep so he did not see them off.

The ride home was quiet and neither of them spoke about what they learned. The thought of what Mr. Sealey told Meena kept circulating in her head and had her on edge for days to come.

Chapter Eleven

Her sister was extremely busy and did not have any time to talk about much since they left the Sealey's home. Dustie was Acting Principal and her school was taking part in a festival so preparation had consumed all her time.

Present at the festival would be the mayor, the police, soldiers, marching bands and maybe the Prime Minister would be there. Meena was one of the honorary guest speakers and she wanted a special outfit to wear for the occasion.

Early next morning she woke Nola from her bed. She told her she would be at her shop in one hour's time. What Nola did not know was that Meena was going to stay until the job was finished. She had time on her hands since she had a few days off from work.

Her cab was driven by Ping and he loved to talk. People avoided Ping's cab like the plague whenever they had a headache because it was never a quiet ride. He usually talks politics, youths of today and religion. There was always a controversial subject that left the passengers angry.

His cab was known as the 'quarrel shop'. That morning was no different. She personally did not mind since he chose a subject she like, 'logging'.

Two corners after she got in, a truck loaded with huge dangerous looking logs, was in front of them. It drove in the middle of the road with little room for others to pass. Ping swung the rearview mirror where he could see her then said :

"Miss you see how they are stripping the forest? That is no good. Everyday on this road I see ten to fifteen trucks loaded like that."

Meena knew he was exaggerating but before she could reply a man seated directly behind him said:

"That isn't true. Maybe a truck or so a week but not all that what you are saying."

Ping was fueled by that statement and he shouted:

"You calling me a liar? I am telling you what I witnessed. I am on this road everyday so I know what I am talking about," stated Ping.

"Oh shut up man! Like you want to bring me deaf! Every time is the same thing with you, talk, talk, talk! I don't know why I put myself in this predicament and travel in this old car for," said the lady next to Ping.

Meena was happy to be in the back seat at the opposite end of them.

The conversation took on a new slant as Ping skillfully passed the truck and everyone was agreeing that he could really drive. Then it was smooth sailing until they reached their destination.

She hesitantly got out then got back in. She found she felt a little scared that day. She wasn't looking forward to meeting up with Ruby so she paid him to take her to Nola's sewing shop, which was three blocks away.

As she got out, Nola was crossing the street with her signature brown bag in her hand, which concealed something. Meena pretended she did not see and greeted her:

"Hi Nola. It's so good to see you looking absolutely wonderful this morning."

She was nicely dressed and really looked pretty that day.

"Thank you very much Meena for that compliment," she said, as she slipped the small bag into her purse. She continued, " Sometimes you just have to try and sometimes I do and other times I fail. So what can I do for you today?" she said sounding very cherry(happy) as she opened the shop.

Meena took out her fabric with the style and showed it to her. She had it drawn. She almost never uses a fashion book since she believes her attire must always be one of a kind.
"I love it. It would look great on you when it is finished. So you'll pick it up tomorrow?"

"No, today"

. "Well you go and take care of your other business and come back in three hours. By then it would be finished," said Nola.

"I have no business to take care of so I am going to wait," replied Meena.

"You gonna do what?" asked Nola, surprised.

"I am going to wait. You are not going to do me like what you did the last time, remember?"

She blushed and said:
"Okay missy, make yourself comfortable."

Meena asked her the cost and was charged a little more than expected. She paid Nola since she knew Nola would do an excellent job since she was sober. Yes the operative word was 'sober', and she would be until Meena's outfit was sewn.

"First we shall eat," said Meena as she cleaned up a little section on a table and spread a napkin. She took out three enormous whole wheat sandwiches with baked chicken, tomatoes, lettuce, and peppery mango chutney nicely ladled between and two big bottles of ice-cold homemade Mauby(a drink made from the bark of a tree).

"Two are yours and one is mine," said Meena.

"Thank you so much Meena. You would not believe I did not have breakfast as yet."

"I thought so because it's real early in the morning and neither did I," said Meena.

After Nola finished eating, she took the fabric and did her thing. Meena occupied herself with reading and doing puzzles. In two and a half hours Nola was almost done. Meena then decided to have a heart to heart talk with her.

"Nola, I want to have a straight talk with you. I hope you'll hear me out.

"I know what you are going to tell me but you go ahead," stated Nola

"Why do you drink so much?"

"To drown my sorrows" she replied.

"What happened?" said Meena.

"Everyone knows, I am surprised you don't know."

"I honestly do not know, and you are aware I am not one who pries."

"Yes that's true. Well it was around two years ago when my husband left me and I turned to the bottle. He drained my bank account. Meena, you know how hard I work for my money then for him to do that. It drove me crazy" she said.

"I am so sorry Nola" said Meena and she felt like crying.

"No do not be. I've gotten over him a long time ago but it is this habit I am trying to kick. I almost lost my house so I had to sell most of my expensive machines to keep paying the mortgage...... when money was not coming in- but I am okay now," said Nola.

"You are not okay. Have you taken any steps to get rid of this problem?"

"No, not really."

"Then what are you going to do?"

"I honestly do not know. All I do know is that I want my life back."

"You know what Nola I am going to call the Alcohol Anonymous group and get some information for you. But in the mean time, you've got to fight the desire girl."

"I am aware of that but it's so hard at times. My body craves for it especially if I start to become anxious. I am so ...." and her voice trailed away with a sigh.

Meena encouraged her and chit chatted for a while and spruced her spirits up until she was finished with her outfit. It fitted superbly and she gave her a generous tip for that. Meena left quite happy and totally satisfied with how things went so far.

Chapter Twelve

On her way home, Meena bought a huge bunch of flowers, some fruits and other knick knacks. She turned down a street that she hardly ever went to and found some ceramic frogs that would go well in the little rock garden she was trying to build. The shop was a home decorator's dream. It was filled with ornaments of all kinds. There were beautiful waterfalls, chandeliers, crystals and oriental rugs. She knew she had to bring her sister to that shop and all the other stores that recently opened on that street.

The owner turned out to be one of the fish vendors that she bought her King fish from. He greeted her with the same warmth and enthusiasm each time she would go to purchase her fish. They spoke for a while and he told her his brother took over the fish business and he was living his dream. He said he always wanted that type of store and he worked hard to get it. She congratulated him on his achievement.

She put a number of things on lay-away and promised she would return on the Saturday to get them. Soon her eyes spied a Silver Sensation jewelry shop that was directly opposite. It was still closed but she browsed the front window and what she saw she loved. Her heart tickled her with sweet anticipation as the shadowy thoughts of all her purchases on Saturday would be great.

She slowly leisurely walked up the street on the opposite side and bought herself a Sour-sop drink. She stood sipping the delicious liquid and debated whether or not to buy two slices of sweetbread or three bags of phulorie from the vendor.

The sunlight shone directly in her face when she became aware someone in a pink mini dress coming down the street swinging her hips from side to side. She paid no attention to who it was until the person stopped right in front of her and said to the vendor:
" Two slices of sweet bread and three currant rolls."

Ruby stood so close to Meena that she could smell her deodorant. She stepped back and looked at her. Ruby said nothing and paid for her items. She turned slightly away from her as she opened a lovely pink leather bag. Meena wished she could've seen what she was hiding in it. Ruby then took a backward step close up to Meena upon the pretense she was trying to see in the vendors showcase. She did it in a flash and was gone as she danced down the street because no one Meena knew ever walked that way.

Meena asked the vendor:
"Do you know her?"

"Yes," she said then continued, "I mean she comes here every day and buys her pastries and leave. She never says anything and it's been over three months since she's been patronizing me."

The vendor soon became busy with customers as Meena relived the moments that just passed by. She wondered what that woman's problem was. Does she hate her? Does she really have a thing for her according to what Mr. Sealey said? Or is she imaging it all? If he is right, she knew they would clash one of these days if she continued to provoke her. She looked down the street and saw that Ruby had boarded a cab, for another town, and she felt relieved.

Meena hurried off to pay her phone bill without buying anything from the vendor. She heard cheups as she walked off since she held up the line and did not purchase. She ignored it and knew there was always another vendor she could patronize.

An hour later she had four parcels and one was a bit heavy so she stood to adjust it. Out of nowhere she heard:
"You need help Meena. All that shopping in so little time," said her tormentor, Ruby.

Now what do you want?" snarled Meena.

"Absolutely nothing my dear. I only observed you having a difficult time with your parcels so I commented," said Ruby, with mock sweetness.

"Then why not just say, can I help you," said an aggravated Meena.

"Me! Not me. I am dressed to sexy to help anybody with parcels. You bought it so struggle with it. No help from me honey," Ruby said spiteful.

Meena felt she could have pulled off her belt and give Ruby the whipping of her life as she stood before her with that sarcastic look on her face.

"Is that a real Gucci purse you have there? I heard it's nine hundred. How much you paid for yours? Did you buy it in the city or when you traveled? She maccociously(inquisitively) asked.

If Meena had answered her there and then, she knew she definitely would have sinned her soul and probably be down on her knees for the next week in sackcloth and ashes begging for forgiveness, so she remained quiet for Ruby's sake.

"It seems like you don't want to be my friend Meena."

"No I don't!" replied Meena.

"Well I want to be your friend- miss social social, drinking coconut water with straw."

Meena began to tap her foot on the ground because her patience began to escape like a deflating balloon and she wished for a cab to come quickly. Whether it is Ping or Snail, she would be gone.

"I heard you're the owner of a school for special kids. It must be nice working with kids" Ruby said calmly.

Yes" answered Meena completely shock.

"It was my dream to become a teacher but circumstances did not allow me to pursue that course," Ruby said, sounding a little disappointed. "But sometimes things do not always work out as we plan, right Meena?"

"Yes," replied Meena, totally disbelieving her ears.

A cab came along and she signaled the driver who acknowledged by nodding. Ruby followed Meena as she went towards the taxi and said:

"Those parcels look really heavy. So what exactly you have in them? Please just give me a quick peek," she begged.

Meena simply stared at her in amazement.

"Okay, I know you won't tell me so have a nice evening. Oh and when you are buying your silvers, get a necklace with a huge flower like the one you wore for your anniversary last year." She gave Meena a dazzling smile and said, "I'll see you on Saturday," as she swayed in the opposite direction.

Those parting words left Meena shaken. For her anniversary she and her husband went to an exclusive restaurant in the city and she didn't recall ever seeing Ruby. As a matter of fact it was only recently she have begun to actually notice her. How in the world she knew Meena was looking at silver jewelry?

She concluded that Ruby was a raving lunatic, psycho or super intelligent. She just did not want to know, but as usual, that was a lie.

Chapter thirteen

Meena made it home without incident and hurriedly prepared dinner before the girls returned home from school. Her sister was still busy with her assignment. Meena decided not to call since their conversations often took hours to come to an end. Three times that evening she made an attempt to pick up the phone . On the fourth she reasoned, assignment or no assignment, she needed to speak to her. So she quickly dialed her number.

"Hello," said Dustie.

"I know you are busy but I have something to tell you. Could you spare me a little time?" Meena asked.

"Sure, what is it? Don't tell me you met you know who."

"Yes I did, and it seems it's exactly like I thought. This woman is crazy!

"What made you say that?"

"Early this morning I saw her and she came and stood close too me. So close that I smelled her."

"What! Are you joking?"

"No! I am dead serious. She bought her stuff and pretended like she did not see me then she took off down the street. Well she danced down the street."

"Dance you say!"

"Yes, in other words, she was wine'in(walking with an exaggerated swing in the hips) going down the street in a pink mini dress. You got it!"

"Repeat that for me again," urged Dustie.

Meena repeated and they laughed for an entire three minutes. When she was able to catch her breath she said:

"There was more"

"Go ahead, I am listening," said Dustie as she laughed in between.

"I was struggling with my parcels and all what she was interested in was knowing how much I paid for my Gucci bag. I got angry and asked her why don't she ask me if she could help and you won't believe what was her reply," said Meena. She continued "I can't even begin to guess so tell me."

"You buy it so struggle with it," and "I'm dressed too sexy to help anybody."

Her sister laughed so hard that she had to hold the phone away from her ears. Meena was infuriated as the scene played back in her mind but she remained cool.

"Meena girl, I am sorry but you know the sense of humor I have."

"She even called me social for drinking my coconut water with a straw, as if that is any concern of hers."

"You know you are social," stated Dustie.

"Umm I admit just a little but that is my business. Just when I thought it was going to get worse her personality changed to one so sweet. She told me she wanted to become a teacher .Can you believe it?"

"You mean she was coherent and logical?"

"Yes, totally."

"That's strange."

"You think that was strange then listen to this. I was about to go into the taxi and she wanted to know what was in the parcels. She actually begged me."

"You're sure you heard right?"

"Perfectly sure."

"The final nail was placed when she told me as I buy my silvers choose a necklace with a big flower like what I wore for my last anniversary.

Now tell me where this woman was hiding when I celebrated my anniversary. Then she grinned and left".

Dustie began to laugh again. She coughed and screamed with laughter so much that she had to hang up the phone to go to the bathroom.

A half an hour later Meena's phone rang and it was Dustie. She apologized for laughing again and Meena assured her it was not a problem. Many times Dustie would come to tell her about some mishap she had, looking for sympathy and she would have a field day of laughter instead.

Meena remembered a particular day Dustie left looking really nice. She was going to a concert and wore this cute long hair titian color wig. She looked like Beyonce.

When she came back she looked totally different. She told her at the entrance to the venue persons started to push and she got caught up in it. She had to hold on for dear life unto the edge of the gate. When the pushing was over, her shades and wig was all gone trampled to the ground plus she had a bruise on her neck from where someone had held on to her jersey(t shirt) so as not to get caught up in the tidal wave of pushers. Fortunately for Dustie, she had a head tie in her purse.

Meena found that to be so funny that she laughed until tears ran down her cheeks. So she understood Dustie's sense of humor although it could be a bit cruel but they never held a deep grudge against one other when situations like that arose.

The perfect time presented itself on the phone to ask about the conversation between her and Mrs. Sealey.

"Dustie, remember you did not tell me what you and Mrs. Sealey spoke about."

"That is drama all by itself. Do you not know she and Mr. Sealey are not married?"

"No, that's not true."

"Yes she told me so herself. She has been living with him for eight years.

"But he is married. I used to hear about a Mrs. Sealey although I'd never met her".

"The original Mrs. Sealey left him ten years ago. She went to England to help her daughter with her children but never returned."

"Hello! Mr. Sealey is a very religious man."

"That is true. He even conducts a bible class. Mrs Sealey said nobody knows that they are not married and she thinks they are hypocrites to let persons believe that. They moved into that neighborhood pretending to be man and wife and he even bought her an engagement and wedding band which she wears."

"I saw the lovely set of sparklers on her fingers. But that is so wrong!" Meena now understood the slight jerking of the hand from his, what it meant.

"Would she leave it like that?" ask Meena.

"I don't think so. She is planning to tell him to take steps to marry her or she would tell the church and would leave. Just recently his married wife has started to communicate with him so she feels insecure. I told her to stick to her plans and do what she thinks is right for her.

"I hope she goes through with it," said Meena.

"I myself feel a little skeptical about it since she confessed to me she loves him so much, as she puts it 'like life itself.'

"Well, for her sake, I hope she goes through with her decision" emphasized Meena.

"So what are you going to do on Saturday?"

"I do not know. I will call Brenda in the morning to see if I could put off our plans for another time," replied Meena.

They then promised to see the next day as she hung up the phone.

That night Meena double checked all of the locks, for it was only the kids and her at home. Her husband was out at work for the next week. She also made sure her dogs were loose that night.

She had a restless sleep and it was entirely devoted to Ruby. She dreamt that Ruby ran after her with a lasso, would catch her and try to take away her hand bag. She would not give it up so they kept struggling for it throughout the night.

Meena awoke around four o'clock that morning fighting with her pillow. She hated nightmares. They left her with a silent headache and sensitive eyes. She got up made herself a cup of mint tea and turned on the TV. She neither saw nor heard anything since her mind was taken over with the thoughts of Ruby. She had to speak to someone so she dialed Bev number.

"Hello," she replied groggy.

"It's Meena Bev. I am so sorry for waking you at this time of the morning."

"I am happy you did since it is almost time for me to get up. Its not all that early. It's five thirty and I am out of bed by six. So what's up?"

"I do not know where to start but I have a problem. Do you know Ruby Brown?"

"Yes I know her. Her house is two blocks away from where my sister lives"

"I think something is wrong with her. She is a psycho. I think she is stalking me because when ever I go to Sangre Grande, she would show up right where I am and she seems to know certain things which I believe is not so coincidental."

"She is employed- how come you are always seeing her? On what days do you see her?" replied Bev.
"So far this past Friday and on Monday."

"It must have been her day off. However she does not work on a Saturday. She is a Fire Woman(Officer)."

"A what!' Meena shouted in disbelief.

"That was my same expression when I found out". Bev laughingly said.

"It was a rainy day and ear splitting thunder could of made a big man cry (thunder was so scary.). Everyone was running for cover where ever they could have found it. It was raining like peas (lots of rain). The streets were flooding and someone was walking by swinging her hips from side to side. It was Ruby and she knows me really well. I was working at another hospital when I helped deliver her still born baby".

That piece of news made Meena feel a little sad for her. That was the first time she felt connected to Ruby. She wondered if that somehow had her a little bit messed up. Bev brought her back to the present as she continued:

"So when she saw me she stopped to ask me why was I out in such bad weather condition".

"Did she have on rain boots?"

"Yes she did because if she didn't then I would've thought she was mad."

"Anyway a man standing next to me commented to another, Ruby was a Firefighter. I shouted exactly what you said not believing him."

"But that is not proof that she really does that job."

"True, but let me tell you what I saw with my own eyes."

"I was spending the weekend at my sister's home when her neighbor's house caught on fire. We rushed over to see what we could have done to help before the Firemen arrived. Two women officers came along with them and worked as hard alongside the men until they put out the fire. When they were through the women removed their helmets. Ruby and I saw each other the same time. My expression was one of surprise because she said:
"Close your mouth, it's me Ruby."

"As they left she saluted me. That girl does things to shock you but she is harmless," said Bev.

"Bev I honestly think otherwise where I am concern. I have plans to meet Brenda on Saturday to go to the fish market. Ruby heard and I believe she would be hiding somewhere to join us along the way."

"You keep calm. I am working late Saturday evening so all three of us would meet somewhere. Call and let me know. If she shows up you would have the opportunity with us backing you to confront her about her behavior" said Bev.

Thank you so much Bev for listening and I definitely will give you a call," Meena said, feeling much braver than when she had gotten up.

They hung up and Meena went about the next few days in quiet contemplation about how exactly she would respond to Ruby when she showed up. This situation had left her drained and she knew she had to deal with it once and for all before she became a nervous wreck.

Chapter Fourteen

Arrangements were made and when Saturday morning came Meena was up and ready. Her stomach was filled of butterflies(terribly nervous). She took her time getting ready not realizing how extremely beautiful she looked. Her chocolate brown skin glowed against her red backless dress. Her huge single braid swung to one side as her beautiful slanted eyes looked smoky and mysterious. From her entry to the cab and on her way to meet her girlfriends, she heard the low seductive whistles of men as they complimented her on how attractive she looked.

Normally she would have smiled and politely say a "thank you" but today she paid little heed to what was said. Her mind was preoccupied with what she had to do. She wondered if things would go smoothly or if a fight might break out between Brenda and Ruby. She wondered if Brenda had the vaguest idea how strong Ruby was. She thought about turning back since she was one of those who never liked to be embarrassed but she knew no matter how she felt, she had to go.

It was a soothing morning. The sun felt warm and comfortable on her skin as the cool breeze enveloped her body. Meena and her girlfriends planned on meeting at a café to have breakfast together. Roasted bake and fried shark was on the menu but the way she felt she knew she would not partake.

From the distance she saw them waiting for her. Everyone looked absolutely gorgeous and sexy, and, as she got closer, they ran towards her in little shuffles. She suddenly remembered this scene replaying in her mind when she was five, only it was Ruby. As she came towards her, she tripped and fell and all their classmates began to laugh. Meena had bent to look at Ruby's bruised knee and was pushed away.

Brenda and Bev told her something that penetrated her subconscious mind as they hugged.
"I'm sure we're not going to the fish market today the way we're dressed," said Brenda, with a giggle. She was dressed in a nice khaki short skirt and yellow top that plunged at the neck line. Her gold necklaces added the look of royalty.

"Absolutely not," said Bev, who was dressed in a white halter back and long white jeans pants, that looked stunning against her cream skin.

Dusty couldn't make it since she was taking care of CeCe, who had a slight fever. Meena felt a momentary twinge of guilt since she never told her sister she had met Bev. But she quickly overcame that feeling. She knew she did not have to face the drama that might have occurred had they met each other again.

In the Bamboo Café, they had a good time. Meena passed on the eats but had a fresh glass of half crushed sweet pineapple that took her nerves away. They joked, reminisced, and shared secrets. They even made a pact that every months end, they would meet to have a Girl's day out.

Meena excused herself and went to the powder room. Upon returning she overheard a conversation that caused her to hide behind the door and eavesdrop.

"When are you going to tell her?" asked Bev.

"I haven't had the opportunity as yet," said Brenda.

"Remember we can't spring that surprise on her. So it's better you tell her as soon as she comes back," said Bev.

"Okay, I'll do it. I just hope she says yes," Brenda said quietly, while looking around.

Meena's curiosity was spooked. She wondered what they wanted to ask her and hoped she'd say yes to. She came back smiling and said :
"Sorry for taking so long girls. Did you all notice what a beautiful day it is? She tried to make small talk to mask the fact that she had overheard their conversation.

"So Brenda what is on the agenda today? I would sure like to do a little shopping. There is this little jewelry store I would like to visit again," said Meena .

"First, as a surprise, we would like to take you to a show. It is in the Community Center and it is starting in half an hour," said Brenda.

"Well let's go," said Meena, as she stood up.

"Meena, it is put on by The Fire Service and Ruby would probably be there. The good thing is that we will be there too" said Brenda .

Meena was silent. She did not want to go into Ruby's realm.

"Would you please please come with us, Meena? I am a member of 'Save The Forest Association' and I have tickets for the show. You have nothing to fear. We will be close by and watching for Ruby's shadow. I promise," beseeched Brenda.

"I am not so sure about that," said a hesitant Meena.

"I promise I would be right by your side girl. Besides, it's a nice show and if you decide to go, you'll see what I mean," assured Bev, as she held Meena's hands.

Meena thought it over for a while and decided to go since it made no sense in being a coward. A confrontation would happen at some point in time so was best to approach it head on, she reasoned.

They left the café with Bev being the designated driver. Upon their arrival, Meena was surprised to see hundreds of persons at the event. Her eyes scanned and rescanned the crowd for that familiar figure but there was no sign of her. Meena breathed a sigh of relief and focused her attention on the occasion.

Booths were set up with pamphlets that gave information about the cycle of devastation that occurs when the forests are stripped. She marveled at the wealth of knowledge printed on a flyer given out by a little girl dressed in butterfly suit.

She became so absorbed in reading and became startled when someone said: "Nice to see you here miss". It was Ping. They had a wonderful chat. She got some background information about the organization and was thrilled to find out Ping was one of the organizer of the event. He told her the organization's hope was to arouse the awareness of how delicate the cycle of the forest was and showed humans that when they destroyed it they were actually killing themselves.

She parted company with Ping found her other friends and they took their seats. Meena was seated in the middle which made her feel really secure. She relaxed and thoroughly enjoyed the program.

The most dramatic scene came when a forest was depicted being burnt to the ground .The cries of the animals, as they raced for their lives, was soul rendering. The river that ran through that forest was dried up –the fish were gone and the birds stood dying on the banks from hunger.

The crowd applauded as the curtains fell. Everyone left with misty eyes. The ladies were deep in thought as they passed a napkin around. The actors mingled with the crowd. People were hugged and they spoke to everyone who had questions. Bev and Brenda were hugged by a bear and monkey which made them giggle. It delighted Meena to watch her friends have fun and she remembered their school days as a weak smile crossed her face.

She then got herself a drink and was sipping it slowly when a bird hugged her tight and said
"Good to see you enjoyed the show Meena. I was surprised when I saw the three of you sitting there. Are they your backup? Do you think they could handle me? I could easily bench press your weight Meena," she stated as she dragged her hands on Meena's bag tugging slightly at the fringes.

The bird disappeared in the crowd. Meena was left breathless and shaken. Her drink had dropped to the ground not being aware it left her hand. She looked at Bev who stood a little distance away from her, completely absorbed in what a deer was telling her. Meena could not believe the encounter that had just taken place. This time she truly believed Ruby was a psycho and she was determined to bring the situation to an end.

Meena stood with a look on her face that read: 'what just happened here!?

Bev glanced over and saw her and hurried over.

"What's wrong Meena? Are you alright? It is her again, isn't it? Queried Bev, as she signaled Brenda over.

Brenda rushed over and immediately said:

"What did she do to you? You know what? I am taking this woman down today!" she swore through her teeth. Did you see where she went?"

Meena pointed to a group of actors dressed as birds. Brenda hurried over and had an animated conversation with the group. She rushed back when she was unable to find her.

"I am so sorry Meena. We tried to avoid this. It is unbelievable she could come right under our noses and upset you like this' said an apologetic Brenda.

Let us get out of here and take Meena to a place where she can relax," said Bev

"Relax? You think she could relax with that psycho on the loose, " said Brenda, as she referred to Ruby.

They continued to speak about Meena as if she was not there. Meena kept quiet as she formulated a plan in her mind. She was determined to find out where Ruby lived and pay her a visit. It really was not a good idea but she had to do something and fast. First she had to hatch a scheme as to how to get rid of them without suspicion. Meena got up, smiled, and then held both their hands.

"Let's go and have something to drink, and do our shopping. We are not going to let her upset our plans. It's too beautiful a day to waste," said a convincing Meena.

"That sounds nice to me. I am sure she is over there somewhere looking at us," said Brenda accusingly.

"Where? You think it is one of those?" asked Bev and started to move in the direction of some bears.

"No, Bev, no. Let's just go. No harm was done and I am a bit thirsty," said Meena, trying to divert her attention. After a last glance around, they left.

Meena put up her best pretense and completely enjoyed herself. Her girlfriends tried every little trick to try to draw Ruby out, which they thought she was not aware of. They left her all alone at times pretending to be looking at something but kept her under discreet observation.

They went to the silver jewelry store and it was great. Meena purchased two sets, one of Turquoise and the other Garnet.

In the store there was a reserved section where customers could be seated. There were lots of books filled with pictures of exquisite jewelry on hand. It took a lot of time to go through all those catalogs. An attendant was on hand to bring what interested those buyers and a jeweler was at their disposal to make any needed adjustments.

Meena coaxed them to sit there while she continued to browse on the outside. She checked in every ten minutes or so and when they became comfortable enough she would slip away. As soon as their interest became focused on a particular tray of diamond jewelry, she seized her opportunity. She gave a note to an attendant and paid her to deliver it only when her friends were about to leave the store. In the note she thanked them for being there for her but she had to settle the matter by herself.

Before she darted out, she checked in as usual and showed them what she had purchased. They all behaved like children in a candy store all giggles with 'oohs' and 'aahs'. They became absorbed in what they purchased so Meena made a beeline for the door. She made one backward glance before she slipped through and screamed in the fright. There stood Brenda two steps away looking at her.

"You thought you had us fooled. We knew what you were up to a long time ago but played along with it," said Bev.

I knew you were trying to ditch us so I told Bev we would keep an eye on you. So what were you up to missy?" asked Brenda

Meena laughed a nervous laugh. "I gave that clerk over there a note to give you as soon as you were about to go through the door," she said, removing some of the attention from her.

They turned and look at the clerk who was busy attending to other clients and not even aware they had gotten up. Brenda went over and retrieved the note. Meena suspected she deliberately did that to see if she told a lie.

"I think it's time we had lunch. I am in the mood to have lobster today. Is that good for everybody? It's my treat," said a jolly Bev.

On the way to the lunch spot, Meena stopped to admire some lovely fabric displayed in a window when Bev and Brenda came running back in her direction. They gave her 'the don't speak' sign and pulled her in a doorway.

"We saw her. She is right over there. She is sitting in the Sea food lounge all by herself and I am going to tackle her," said Brenda and handed over her parcels to Bev.

"I want to do this my way," stated Meena. She felt a rush of fright, excitement and calmness all at the same time.

Meena turned the corner very cautiously and there she sat all absorbed in something she was writing. Her hair was pulled up in one with a beautiful afro puff that gave little glances of pearls that were stuck between them. She wore three interwoven strands of pearls. She looked like a beautiful swan. Meena was sure Ruby had sensed she was being watched and probably guessed who it was. Her eyes were drawn to her muscled arm and she wondered how strong she really was. Ruby was busy writing in a small book that looked like a diary.

She had a light blue hand bag that matched her armless ruffled short top. She tucked the bag close to her body as if to reassure herself it was there. Meena wondered what was hidden in her bag that made her act that way. All those thoughts raced through her mind as she slowly and quietly moved towards her.

Meena felt like a lion stalking its prey and would soon get the reward. There was an underlying pureed rush of excitement that had her sweating due to the upper hand she had for once. She was so close that if she wanted to she could read what was written. Meena came around to the front of her.

"Hi Ruby, it is good to see you. Looks like you're enjoying your writing," said Meena with satisfaction. Ruby shook and hurriedly closed her diary putting it away in her bag.

"Hello Meena, you look great," she said with an enchanting smile. "Were you standing for a long time behind me?" asked Ruby staring straight at Meena's bag.

"No, I saw you and I decided to come and say hi to you," said Meena.

"That is strange since you are the one that tries to avoid me every living time we meet," said Ruby accusingly.

"May I sit if that is ok with you?" asked Meena.

"Of course you can. What is all this about? Pray do tell me," said Ruby, with an outrageous head movement and attitude.

"I want to know why you are stalking me and do I have to get the cops involve in this," said Meena going straight to the point.

"Me stalking you? Never! This is craziness. Meena all I ever wanted to be was your friend and you have resisted since childhood," she said accusingly.

"Now tell me how am I guilty of that since I have vague recollection of it," replied Meena in a manner not to hurt her feelings.

"You remember the notes I used to pass to you and you would crumple it up and throw it back at me," said Ruby, with her eyes beseeching her to remember.

"I kind of, and if I did that I would thought it was a game you were playing and remember Ruby we probably couldn't write well. Also when you are small, everything is a game or a joke," said Meena, hoping that excuse would pacify her.

"It was no joke for me Meena," she replied.

"I humbly apologize for that. Please forgive me Ruby," replied a sincere Meena.

"But what about the time I bent to look at your bruise knee and you push me away," Ruby ranted on.

"You are sure you have that story right? Wasn't it you who laughed at me! Stated a confused Meena.

"It wasn't me. It was the other kids," she said and her eyes fastened once more on Meena's bag.

Meena did not miss a beat. She caught every look at her bag, the slight hesitation to reach out to touch it and the way she held hers tight if she happens to glance at it which was more often than usual. But the time now was to get answers to questions.

"Ruby how come you were in the same place where I celebrated my anniversary?" asked Meena, almost daring her to come up with an excuse.

"That was pure co-incidence" she laughed, and then continued, "I also work as a part time caterer and I did two anniversaries that day. Yours happen to be one of them. When I recognized it was your party, I hid most of the time in the kitchen," said Ruby beginning to sound a little bit bored.

"What's up with the pretense you do not see me then come in real close then go pass straight? Do you know that is nerve racking. And what it is about not helping me when I needed your help? It's like you become another person sometimes," Meena fired at her trying to bring the interrogation to end.

"My intention was always to speak to you but I always get cold feet for whatever reason. And I deliberately said those things about not helping you because you looked at me with disgust in your eyes. That day you roused my anger," Ruby said, looking uncomfortable.

She looked, around and asked "Where is Brenda and Bev? Brenda brings out the brute in me, especially when she refers to me as a twig she'd love to beat" said Ruby broodingly.

Meena erupted into laughter and even Ruby joined in. She then became very serious then said,
"I am very strong and she cannot handle me. Now where are they Meena?"

"They are somewhere, perhaps still shopping," said Meena somewhat stretching the truth.

Ruby looked around then directed her attention back to Meena . She complimented Meena on the way she was dressed, all the while her eyes were fastened on the bag.

A waitress brought across two large glasses of ice cold coconut water and told them it was compliment from two friends. She then pointed in their direction. It was an open air restaurant and both Bev and Brenda were sitting under a straw umbrella sipping their drinks and waving at them.

Ruby put down her glass after a long sip and looked at Meena's bag with such intensity that she pulled it unto her lap.

"I want to see what's in your bag Meena," stated Ruby. Neither her voice nor her expression gave anything away but the rise and fall of her deeply exposed bosom did.

Meena's mind was on the same level and in the same vortex. It was like if at that moment nothing existed except them and their desire.

"Show me yours and I will show you mine" were the words that escaped from Meena's lips barely above a whisper.

As if in slow motion Ruby took her hand bag off her shoulder unzipped it and opened it up for Meena to see. Meena did the same. They slid their hands over pretended no interest then snuck their hand in each other's bag.

Meena lifted her eyes and saw both Brenda and Bev standing with their hand over their mouth with an expression that read 'oh my god what are they doing'. The impulse was to keep searching the bag. She did not care what they thought or said at that moment.

Meena found Ruby's diary to be a treasure-it was like a doorway to her soul .The last few entries were fascinating. It said 'what can I do to become her friend. I blew it again today because those two buzzards were around. I wonder when I will get the opportunity to see what miss pompous carries in her bag. In the middle of the diary she wrote 'I love J' and the rest of the sentence she erased. Her bank account and investments were enormous.
  Meena felt a bulge between the lining and the bag itself. She extracted the paper and opened it. It contained drawings of lots of things. Written in the end were; All this belong to M but was now mine. Meena felt a rush of nerves that made her feel cold. She slipped the note to the ground and made eye contact with Brenda to pick it up.

Ruby was looking at every family photo, read every scrap of paper and became absorbed with two letters she had in her bag. Meena knew she had some very sensitive things in there but was happy on that morning she had decided to use a bag that did not contain her personal note book. Meena looked at Ruby who then leaned back with a satisfied smile on her face and her eyes glint with knowledge. Everything from Meena's bag was on the table and the pockets were turned inside out. She wondered what she did that for only to see she had also emptied Ruby's personals which included her wallet, money and credit cards.

They looked at each other and smiled nervously. They were sweating. Meena knew where she was and wanted to escape. Bev and Brenda replaced the belonging to their respective bags and hand them over to their owners. No mention was made of what had transpired for the entire evening.

Meena saw a tiny paper stuck at the edge of her bag and before she could examine it carefully it was snatched out of her hands. It was a picture of cut out eyes and it looked quite familiar. Ruby stared at her was certain she saw her muscle bulged. She put it down as her imagination in order to enjoy herself. They laughed shared little secrets then realized Ruby was not in their category.

The evening closed with promises of month end returns to the café and keeping in touch. They hugged and stood up to leave when Brenda's bag slipped from her shoulder and fell to the ground. They all reached to help at the same time. Lying halfway out of the bag was a gun and binoculars. Ruby hastily got up and ran away. Brenda secured her stuff and looked like a deer caught in the headlights. Bev held her hand and hurried her away and with one back ward glance she saw Brenda was speaking on a communicator. Meena did not know what to make of anything, she needed time to think, probably investigate. She pulled her hand away from Bev and began to run since she did not know if she had a deep secret also.

Index

ah….a

bus-up shot……thin flat pastry like bake…when shaken falls to pieces

big shots…….rich folks

Calypso….type of commentary song

cut that boy's tail….. give immediate discipline

chutney……grated mango or tamarind sauce with pepper

chutney music….indigenous to T/dad evolved from rhythmic East Indian music

cheups……suck your teeth to show displeasure

dat…………………that

doubles…two seasoned fried bakes that sandwich curried garbanzo beans and other niceties

de....the

every fox and its mother....everyone you can think of

fix her..... chastise to the fullest degree

fortnight.....two week period

mix ....mixed race

mauby... drink made from the bark of a tree

making small talk.....being polite by striking up conversation

need turpentine....they should move faster(just a saying)

playing the monkey......doing nonsensical things that could get one in trouble

ruffle your feather....aggravate

social.....holding oneself slightly aloof

sour-sop....fruit from which milky drink and ice-cream is made

stupidness......nonsense

www.ingramcontent.com/pod-product-compliance
Lightning Source LLC
Chambersburg PA
CBHW060113260626
47160CB00005B/1882